Devil's Island

(Matt Drake #20)

By

David Leadbeater

Copyright 2018 by David Leadbeater
ISBN: 9781791975791

All rights reserved. No part of this publication may be reproduced, distributed, or transmitted in any form or by any means, including photocopying, recording, or other electronic or mechanical methods, without the prior written permission of the publisher/author except in the case of brief quotations embodied in critical reviews and certain other non-commercial uses permitted by copyright law. All characters in this book are fictitious, and any resemblance to actual persons living or dead is purely coincidental.

This ebook is for your personal enjoyment only. This ebook may not be re-sold or given away to other people. If you would like to share this ebook with another person, please purchase any additional copy for each reader. If you're reading this book and did not purchase it, or it was not purchased for your use only, then please return it and purchase your own copy. Thank you for respecting the hard work of this author.

Thriller, adventure, action, mystery, suspense, archaeological, military, historical

Other Books by David Leadbeater:

The Matt Drake Series
A constantly evolving, action-packed romp based in the escapist action-adventure genre:

The Bones of Odin (Matt Drake #1)
The Blood King Conspiracy (Matt Drake #2)
The Gates of Hell (Matt Drake 3)
The Tomb of the Gods (Matt Drake #4)
Brothers in Arms (Matt Drake #5)
The Swords of Babylon (Matt Drake #6)
Blood Vengeance (Matt Drake #7)
Last Man Standing (Matt Drake #8)
The Plagues of Pandora (Matt Drake #9)
The Lost Kingdom (Matt Drake #10)
The Ghost Ships of Arizona (Matt Drake #11)
The Last Bazaar (Matt Drake #12)
The Edge of Armageddon (Matt Drake #13)
The Treasures of Saint Germain (Matt Drake #14)
Inca Kings (Matt Drake #15)
The Four Corners of the Earth (Matt Drake #16)
The Seven Seals of Egypt (Matt Drake #17)
Weapons of the Gods (Matt Drake #18)
The Blood King Legacy (Matt Drake #19)

The Alicia Myles Series
Aztec Gold (Alicia Myles #1)
Crusader's Gold (Alicia Myles #2)
Caribbean Gold (Alicia Myles #3)

The Torsten Dahl Thriller Series
Stand Your Ground (Dahl Thriller #1)

The Relic Hunters Series
The Relic Hunters (Relic Hunters #1)
The Atlantis Cipher (Relic Hunters #2)

The Disavowed Series:
The Razor's Edge (Disavowed #1)
In Harm's Way (Disavowed #2)
Threat Level: Red (Disavowed #3)

The Chosen Few Series
Chosen (The Chosen Trilogy #1)
Guardians (The Chosen Tribology #2)

Short Stories
Walking with Ghosts (A short story)
A Whispering of Ghosts (A short story)

All genuine comments are very welcome at:

davidleadbeater2011@hotmail.co.uk

Twitter: @dleadbeater2011

Visit David's website for the latest news and information:
davidleadbeater.com

Devil's Island

CHAPTER ONE

In his mind she was already dead.

Her and her two children. The Devil drank tepid water from a paper cup before biting into a ripe plum. He wiped his fingers on a napkin. He watched the woman emerge from school having dropped her children off. He followed her moves, actions, habits.

But that was just on one of his monitors.

Four others were dedicated to different parts of her life. Social media. Web browsing. An appointment calendar. Local events. They were part of a five-strong desktop array that filled the Devil's vision, angled so he could see them all with a quick glance.

"Hey," he shouted into absolute silence. "Take this shit away."

The slave crept in from an outer room, picked up the paper cup and the plum stone, and departed without making the slightest sound. It didn't dare. The rules, and punishments, were clear.

The Devil studied his prey for another few hours, watching her, reading about her, delving into her social media activities, researching the various 'events' she'd marked down as 'going to' or 'interested.'

Which one would offer up the best kill?

After a while, the Devil sat back. That was enough for today. He checked his notes. So far, the Cameron Street event was offering the best opportunity, but he wasn't done yet. There were others to study. He took a moment to gather his thoughts then reached for the large, white encrypted satphone.

"What news from ground zero?" He spoke immediately the call was answered.

"DC is hot. There are humid days. The tourist flow is large. Endless. The streets are packed, unpredictable. I'd say that the whole scenario is just that—unpredictable. Roadworks are everywhere, narrowing options. Luckily, the proposed kill sites are out of the center but still disordered and messy. We're planning on scouting the sites today. The police are effective but underfunded and stretched thin even here."

The Devil waited, but no more information was forthcoming. The news wasn't surprising. On complex jobs like this he always employed a remote two-man team. They would scout the area, work through his kill scenarios, follow the target, and then report back, naming every conceivable hazard, pitfall and surprise they could conjure up. Anything—no matter how petty, juvenile or ambiguous. Basically, their job was to pave the road.

The Devil signed off, sat back and considered scenarios. He'd done this a thousand times. More than that. He was the perfect paradox. The most renowned and anonymous assassin in the world, its greatest contract killer. Renowned only in certain places and to those that passed many tests, used the correct back channels, and offered the name of a sponsor that had used the Devil's specific services before.

Even to those that knew him, knew he existed, he was a bedtime horror story, a campfire terror, concocted to frighten friends and enemies alike.

After all, who would believe that a man existed who, if paid enough, would murder any man or woman in the world and make their deaths look like a terrible, irrefutable accident? Who would believe he'd been doing it for thirty years? Who would believe all the stories—the jet liner he'd crashed over the Pacific for a single-mother kill, the bridge collapse in Japan for an accountant, the nightclub fire for one boy's sister, desperate to take the family inheritance? It was all fiction and conspiracy. Wasn't it?

The Devil lacked any morals and conscience. He had a desk full of gadgets and a remote team. He embraced all new technology as soon as he understood how it made him better at his job. He enjoyed testing every new device.

But the real thrill came at the end, and he always reserved it for himself. The real thrill was in that final kill, that miracle mile when he walked away, leaving the carnage behind and knowing that—though certain police elements suspected his involvement—they would never truly know.

Which brought his thoughts around to Luka Kovalenko and Devil's Island.

"Hey," he summoned the slave again. "Bring more food."

It was going to be a long evening here on Devil's Island. New arrivals were expected. Yes, this was his island, his resting place, but many years ago he'd turned it into a haven for killers and soon after lost almost all control of the place. Lesson learned. The castle was now the only place he and his men were safe. The ragtag clansmen out there could never breach this place.

Clansmen or islanders were his terms for the groups of madmen and killers running amok on his island, living with impunity. The Devil was an orderly man and liked to slot things into orderly boxes.

Moving away from the monitors that encapsulated his newest project in DC, he walked over to the right side of the room. This was his local surveillance wall. The castle bristled with CCTV monitors, many positioned to watch the approaches and the areas outside in case of an attack, but others employed to observe its residents.

The Devil cast a cursory glance over them now. All appeared to be in order. Of course, he didn't have time to keep a constant watch. That was the job of four men stationed on the castle's first floor level that had a similar bank of monitors. The camera he was most interested in surveilled an upper floor room. It would make a noise when the outer doors opened.

Luka Kovalenko had been inside that room for a long time now.

The self-proclaimed Blood King was alone, but nevertheless possessed the savvy and guts to insist he be given one of the only rooms in the castle that wasn't bugged or monitored. Money talked, especially for the Devil right now, and his request was granted. No doubt the evil little monster had brought surveillance testing and dampening equipment with him too. The Devil grudgingly admitted that Kovalenko was exquisitely good at everything he put his mind to.

What on earth was the sneaky Russian bastard up to?

The Devil had followed his recent exploits across London and Paris. It was all a bit noisy, a bit brash, but the Devil understood why. The Blood King was announcing his leadership of the criminal empire. He was taking his father's kingdom back. In one dreadful swoop, he had become the worldwide head of organized crime, a new nightmare figurehead to haunt every government's dreams, and sent a thousand would-be usurpers scuttling back into their filthy dens.

Well done.

Yes, it was grudging praise, but it was still praise. The Devil didn't spread it around. At that moment the slave entered the room, once more bowing and scraping its heels to announce its presence. The Devil didn't acknowledge it in any way. Why would he? It did as it was told, or it suffered horrible consequences. Either outcome didn't bother the Devil.

Soon, he tired of the surveillance feeds and returned to the new project in DC. Remote feeds watched the front of the woman's house, the rear garden, the windows and the two-vehicle garage. A tracker denoted the position of her car and her push-bike twenty-four-seven. She appeared to have no friends. She was relatively new to the area. There were no interior monitors, but the Devil didn't need them—he had access to her internet activity in real time. He never killed anyone at home. It was one of the hardest places to engineer a fatal accident. Far better for a chance encounter in an unfamiliar place, an unfamiliar situation, a one-off, distinct event.

And far better for the Devil if others died at the same time. Their deaths would help dilute the impact of casualties. He'd long since known that multiple fatalities drew far less attention to him than just one.

The woman in question would be one of the easier kills, he thought, even considering the uncertain and unplannable factors that surrounded a public event. But that was what he loved about mothers—they always enhanced their children's days with trips to the park and the mall; they attended shows and parades; they visited local attractions and ate at fast-food outlets.

He smiled. Even under police protection, Johanna Dahl and her two daughters were vulnerable.

CHAPTER TWO

Apart from an enforced plane journey, the SPEAR team took no down time following their exploits in Paris. On landing in DC, they went straight from the airfield to the battle room, their entire focus aimed at finding their abducted friends.

Only hours had passed since they left Paris aboard *Air Force One*.

But they were the most precious hours for Mai and for Luther, for Karin and Dino. By now, Drake knew, his friends could be anywhere on the planet.

There was no time to relax, to come to terms with everything that occurred. More importantly, they couldn't mourn Smyth and Lauren. And the hunt for the new Blood King would have to wait.

Hayden led the way from the plane to a hastily commandeered CIA satellite office within DC. It was convenient, accessible and came equipped with the latest technology. It offered everything they needed to get started.

Inside, they shrugged out of their bulletproof jackets, depositing them on the backs of chairs, across sofas or over the kitchen worktop. They divested themselves of weapons, heaping their well-used guns and knives into a pile and sending Molokai and Kenzie to the armory to organize new ones.

Drake used his arm to sweep the room's only table free of clutter—chip wrappers, used paper cups and plates, magazines, scraps of paper—and placed a top-of-the-range laptop at one end. Alicia brought up a chair.

Dahl studied Kinimaka. "Time to earn that Kona Coffee blend, bro."

"Yeah, yeah."

The big Hawaiian placed a still-hot coffee he'd appropriated from the *Air Force One* staff, next to the laptop and squeezed his bulk into the chair. It was a tight fit and included the precarious grinding of wooden legs. Hayden moved the coffee further away to prevent an accident.

Kinimaka opened the laptop. "Give me some space, guys. This isn't exactly my forte."

"If it helps," Alicia said. "You're all we've got. Karin and Lauren were the real computer whizzes."

"I'm with you." Dahl sat down beside him. "Whatever you need."

Drake blinked at the Swede. "What the hell could a mad bell end do with real technology?"

"He could find the closest second-hand Saab dealership," Alicia suggested.

Dahl glared at them both, knowing their banter was part of the coping process.

Kinimaka logged in and stared at a black screen. "Crap. Where do I even start?"

"What do you know?" Dallas asked. "Start there."

Drake looked over at the newcomer. Dallas was Kenzie's new—and only—employee. Dallas assumed he was being paid but Kenzie wasn't so sure. He was black, well-built and earnest. He was a huge sentimentalist, always reflecting back on the good old times. During the last battle against the Blood King in Paris's American embassy, Drake thought Dallas had seemed a bit overwhelmed, but then he couldn't blame the man. He'd signed on as a new member of Kenzie's band of relic smugglers and, that same day, had ended up fighting in the streets of Paris and giving almost everything to save the life of the President of the United States and his family. Quite the baptism of fire.

Drake offered a sheet of paper and a pen to Dallas. "You'd best write it down, mate," he said. "The Swede struggles with proper languages."

Dahl ignored him. Alicia spoke first. "Mai and the others are being taken to a place called Devil's Island, far from DC. They're being shipped, we believe. It's part of some convoluted plan of Luka Kovalenko's—the new Blood King—although I think I remember him saying he wasn't going to be there."

Drake accepted a can of Pepsi Max from Hayden. "He said he was too busy planning the next attack."

At that moment, Kenzie re-entered the room. "And I know someone else who won't be there," she grinned. "Topaz."

Drake grimaced, remembering Kovalenko's vicious female bodyguard and her brutal end.

Alicia clucked her tongue. "Well some of her will be. You still got her blood on your shirt."

Kenzie deposited eight identical handguns onto the table before dipping her chin and inspecting the front of her shirt. "Guess it'll have to come off." She started unbuttoning.

"Whoa," Dahl cried out. "We're trying to concentrate."

"Do I distract you, Torsten? Anyway, I'm wearing a sports bra."

"No, no," Alicia groaned, peering between her fingers. "Nobody wants to see that."

"Don't worry, Myles. If I wanted you, you'd be putty in my hands."

Alicia leaned over to Drake. "Did she say I'd be pussy in her hands?"

"No!"

Dallas finished his scribbled note and slid it over the table to Kinimaka.

The Hawaiian was clicking away at the keyboard. "I'm reviewing facts I already checked back in Paris," he said. "There was the penal colony of Cayenne in the 19th and 20th centuries, called Devil's Island, in French Guiana. Closed down in 1953. Seventy thousand were sent there, never to escape."

Kinimaka bit a thumbnail. "It inspired the movie, *Papillon*. There was another penal colony close to Panama, called the same. There's an old movie. A song. None of this purports to our Devil's Island."

Drake felt his cellphone vibrate and moved to the back of the room before checking the screen. He'd received too much bad news through his phone—a fact which now gave him a rush of anxiety whenever it rang—but this caller made him intensely happy.

"Yorgi," he said. "Everything okay, mate?"

"Yeah as long as I don't move I'm fine."

"There's a lesson for you. The next time somebody fires two bullets at you, get out of the bloody way."

It was a little early for leg-pulling. Yorgi was silent for a long moment. "I feel so sorry for Archer and Webster," he said. "They saved my life."

"Good soldiers," Drake said, his voice gruff. "Greater men."

"You knew them?"

"Not well. Archer was a pool shark. Webster was a biker. Both were highly regarded and heading for the top." His eyes lost focus. "Either would have been welcome to join the SPEAR team."

"I'm gonna be here another few weeks," Yorgi said after a

pause. "But Matt . . . before I was shot, I found my brothers. My sister. I'm planning their relocation."

"I know," Drake said. "After we find Mai and the others, our next job is heading over there to help you."

Emotion filled the Russian's voice. "Thank you."

"Hey, it's all good. We're family. Also, Hayden has a proposal for all of us. We want you to hear it too."

"What kind of proposal?" Yorgi sounded interested.

"Something life-changing. According to Hayden, it's gonna make everything better, and fresher, and much more fun. I guess we'll wait and see."

"That gives me something to look forward to." Yorgi's voice tailed off with tiredness. Drake said his goodbyes. There would be enough time for their Russian sojourn later.

Returning to the table, he fought off a rush of combined grief and fear for friends lost and missing. "Where are we?"

Hayden looked up. "Dark Web."

"I thought you needed a special kind of computer for that."

"This is a CIA station," Molokai reminded him.

He kicked himself. Of course they'd be set up for that. Chances were, they'd probably invented the Dark Web to keep tabs on criminals and the worst type of predators. Molokai's words, however, made Drake wonder once more about the leper's mysterious past.

One day, he vowed, *we'll find out.*

"This is slow going." Kinimaka scratched his head in frustration. "More so, because I don't know the slang, the right buzz words. I can't work at the correct pace, which is friggin' light speed. The people using this network—the ones that matter—can spot an interloper ten thousand miles away. I'm safer on the forums, using keywords."

"Like with Bing?" Alicia asked.

"No, not really."

Drake watched Kinimaka navigate his way through one of the most horrific networks on the planet. Thirty minutes passed and then an hour. Molokai handed out rifles, spare ammo, knives and grenades in abundance. Kenzie swopped their flak jackets. Dahl rose and grabbed a handful of prepack sandwiches from the refrigerator, followed by bottles of water.

Nobody voiced their worst thoughts but everyone in the room worried that Mai and Luther, Karin and Dino, as time wore on, were being subject to an enemy's whims, an enemy's preferences, and an enemy's failings.

Drake searched for a calm center, but the overwhelming loyalty he felt for every member of the team prevented him from finding it. Before their search for the bones of Odin began years ago, he'd struggled to find his niche in this world, a real sense of belonging. But the friends he'd met since along the way, and in the unlikeliest places on earth, had grounded him, given him a home that felt right. The home that was Team SPEAR.

It was why every hour, every day, he never faltered. Never quit. He turned up, dug in, chased the next mission, never came up for air. SPEAR was his world, his family, and his rightful place in this world. Ever since the quest for the bones of Odin, he'd proved it every day.

But change always came, no matter if you wanted it to or not. And at any cost. To survive, they would all have to roll with the changes.

Kinimaka clicked his fingers at the screen. "Gotcha."

Hayden looked up from the weapon she was cleaning. "Found something, Mano?"

"Just a small group of mercs chatting in a forum. Not about the island but about some underworld icon they call the Devil. They're arguing the fact that he's real with some others who're just ribbing them. Trolling them, actually."

"Get to the point," Dahl said.

"Yeah, well that kind of is the point. Following 'devil' keywords led me here and then . . . well, I'll read it out: 'We just came from the dude's island, man. He's real.' And: 'We got orders from the Devil. We left the island a few days ago.'"

"It's thin," Hayden said. "But let's go talk to them. Where are they?"

"Salou." Kinimaka frowned.

Hayden did a double take. "Salou? In Spain?"

"It is a coastal town," Kenzie said.

"I know it's a coastal town, but . . . shit."

Dahl tapped the table with his fingers. "What she's trying to say is—it's a long way to go if we're wrong."

Drake wondered if there might be more within the thread. "Keep looking, Mano."

"Yeah, I'm on it, brah."

A few tense moments passed before he spoke again. "I have something but it's obscure. Our three mercs were asked to describe the island. Quote: 'There's an old castle, heavily fortified. A land mass crawling with murderers, all factioned up. A big dock. And, today, a superyacht.'"

"Kovalenko?" Drake asked.

"It's possible."

"It's still a big stretch," Hayden said.

"The conversation's ongoing," Kinimaka said. "They're asked who's on board. Our mercs don't know. They're asked who it belongs to. They don't know. But then they're asked its name. And they reply . . . the *Second Storm*." He paused, looking up.

Dahl was on it. "Which is a play on the old Blood King's

yacht. That was called *Stormbringer*. And Luka is his legacy."

"A second storm." Kinimaka shrugged.

"Anything else?" Dahl asked.

"Only that someone asks them for the island's location. They answer: 'Nobody who leaves ever knows where it is.'"

"That's better," Hayden admitted. "We know Luka was briefly headed to the island. We know he sent our friends there, so must have visited before. With their other comments I think we're safe to assume this is the real Devil's Island."

Drake rose to his feet. "Then let's stop dicking around and find a plane."

There were no arguments.

Salou was a Spanish resort town with long stretches of beach denoted by rocky outcroppings and a busy town center catering for tourists. It was famous for its windsurfing and sunset views just as much as its renowned PortAventura World resort. On seeing the town for the first time, Hayden thought it looked tired—one of those places with incredibly high tourist footfall that hadn't been allowed to primp or embellish or reinvent itself for too many years. Buildings looked in need of paint and care. Shops and restaurants were the same as they had been two decades ago. On the other hand, it was a place that attracted newcomers and romantics alike.

And idling mercenaries, it seemed.

They landed at the airport and walked out into a wall of heat. Sweating, they negotiated a special customs area set up by Spain to accommodate pre-cleared foreign operatives. Hayden now followed Kinimaka along a street lined by market stalls, cheap souvenir shops and cafes. Every few steps they were forced to split and thread their way through droves of locals and tourists. Hayden saw all walks of life in this town. Women clad in bikinis. Shopkeepers wearing thick cardigans. Moped-driving youths delivering goods between souvenir outlets. A hen party squawked by. A British group of lads shouted happily in each other's faces. Noise came from every direction. She was glad when they left the street and Kinimaka turned them into a quieter one.

"Are we close?" Alicia asked.

"Four minutes," the Hawaiian answered.

"Good, 'cause my body clock is telling me it's 2 a.m., not p.m."

"Yeah." Kinimaka nodded. "We should be sleeping."

"Sleep?" Alicia gave him a look of incredulity. "No, dude, we should be shagging."

"Well . . ."

"Are you and Hayden back at it yet?"

Kinimaka brightened to the color of a Hawaiian sunset whilst Hayden grinned. It wouldn't be long. They had been approaching that part of their relationship when Kovalenko hit London and even before that at the end of their chase for the weapons of the gods.

It was worth the wait.

Hayden stayed close, thinking of the enormous proposal she'd be offering them all at the end of this. It was good. It was future proof. Like most of her team, she'd been immersed in action and adventure since she met Matt Drake and Ben Blake at the Library of Congress in Washington DC. Back then, she'd been assigned to Secretary of Defense, Jonathan Gates, as a CIA liaison. The following years had seen her fight through innumerable encounters with good and evil, seeing exuberant life and shocking death. Overall, when she looked back, she felt like she hadn't stopped chasing for a decade.

It was far less than that, and that was part of the problem.

Hayden used to believe that she should be a role model, that she had to live up to the great memory of her father—James Jaye. It had taken many years of hard living and near-death encounters for her to realize that she didn't have to live up to anything.

She only had to be true to herself.

Admit what you want. Embrace change, you might like it. Yes, she'd taken that on board. She wanted Mano Kinimaka. And it would take a huge change to achieve that, which the proposal offered. To her mind, Team SPEAR all wanted something similar.

They would embrace the change, she was sure. They had nothing to lose.

Ahead, Kinimaka slowed and announced they'd arrived at the address. It was a gloomy looking sports bar, off the main street. Hayden's senses were attuned—checking out the environment. The narrow sidewalk running past its front door vanished further down the street, around an acute corner. Molokai was already stalking off, checking it out. There was no roof access from this point. Two run-down shops faced the bar, one selling perfumes and the other selling sporting goods. By the look of them they were small units, offering no rear access. The bar itself was fronted by grimy windows.

Drake was already at the door. "We ready?"

He entered without waiting. Hayden followed fourth in line. They were dressed down for this mission—having convinced the four mercs over the Internet that they were fellow soldiers looking for a little guidance and were willing to fund their next two weeks in sunny Spain in return for some help. Hayden was under no illusions though. Mercs were a tight-knit bunch and would remain tight-lipped. Violence wouldn't be far from the surface. Testosterone was expected.

Inside, four small televisions played sports channels. A long, narrow bar faced them; a wary bartender behind looking up as they entered. A couple of older men sat to the right, nursing beers. Two youths lounged in window seats. To the left, three hard looking men in tight T-shirts stared, narrowing their eyes at the approaching party. They didn't speak as Drake approached.

Everyone carried concealed weapons. Hayden positioned her right hand within reach of her Glock.

"Ey up," Drake said. "We're looking for Ray Harrison."

Hayden tensed. This was the agreed greeting. If the mercs didn't like the situation they would start something now.

A moment of tension passed and then a voice spoke up at their backs. "Hey. I'm Ray Harrison."

Hayden spun. It was one of the older guys who'd been sitting watching TV, regarding them with a smug expression on his face. Clearly, he thought he'd outsmarted them.

Molokai laid a huge hand on the guy's shoulder. "Good to meet you," he boomed in the man's ear.

Harrison turned to look and then flinched away. "What the fuck is that?"

He hurried past Hayden to the table where his own colleagues sat.

Drake placed two hands on its surface and leaned in. "He's our friend. Now, are we good?"

Harrison looked across at his friends before answering.

"We're good. Next time, it'd be better if you mentioned there were eight of you."

"We're not planning on a next time, pal." Drake seated himself at the table. Dahl drew up a chair alongside whilst Kinimaka and Molokai stood at their backs. The sight was intimidating, arranged to lessen the chances of violence.

Harrison nodded at his three colleagues. "That's Rob Brown, Chris Brown and Paul Smith," he said.

Alicia chortled. "Two Browns and a Smith? Come on."

"It's true," the one called Smith said, flashing her a haughty glance.

She held a hand out and flashed all three of them a sarcastic expression. "Hi, Cara Delvigne at your service."

Drake gave her a warning glance whilst the mercs just looked confused. "Don't worry about her," he said. "She's an acquired taste. We just need to talk about Devil's Island."

Harrison leaned back, saying nothing.

Rob Brown answered, "We were kept in a compound near the docks at night. During the day we were given access to the castle, but nothing else. We kept the slaves in line. We unloaded and loaded the ships, keeping an eye on everything. We manned the castle walls just in case the islanders attacked."

Hayden's head filled with a dozen questions.

Drake asked his own before she could open her mouth. "Islanders?"

Chris Brown took that one. "We don't know a hell of a lot. We were there just a few weeks. There's this guy they call the Devil—he owns and runs the place—and a long time ago, presumably when he was less experienced—he brought the worst of the worst there. The most hunted men in the world. He let them live out of sight of the authorities and everyone else. I don't know why. Through the years the numbers grew, and these men started in-fighting. Eventually they formed clans. I think there are four. So now, the Devil lives in his castle by the docks, where twenty-four hours a day he's forced to guard everything he owns. The docks form the only accessible landing area on the island which is obviously why he built the castle there. The rest of it . . ." Brown passed a finger across his neck. "Deadly. Unapproachable."

"Four clans?" Drake replied. "How do they survive?"

"Well, the Marauders have the cliffs to the west. The caves. There are small animals, but also small valleys where they grow food. The Hunters have the big valley, where the food is more plentiful, the land arable. The Creepers have the forest. The Scavengers—the baddest assholes of all—prey on everything else. And they all have the surrounding coastlines, the cliffs, whatever else is there. Maybe they fish. Who knows?"

"How strong are these clans?" Dahl asked.

"Not a clue, bud. Dozens strong, I would say."

"And they never attack the castle?"

"Oh shit, yeah, they attack. But they always lose."

"So far," Harrison put in.

"What do you know about this Devil character?" Molokai asked.

Harrison eyed the giant. "Didn't hear a whole hell of a lot. The other guys kept tight lipped. He's one scary dude and lets it be known on your first day that any trespassing, any breach of trust, or any inquiries into him or his past will be met with extreme prejudice. And he didn't just mean a firing squad or an enforced cliff dive. I saw a kid, only two years a merc, staked out on the beach for days, bleeding out slowly, salt water rushing over his wounds, the hard sun blistering his face. Must have been excruciating, and he was staked right among us, on the walkway from the compound to the docks." He shook his head. "The Devil deserves his title."

"Okay," Hayden understood they wouldn't be learning any more about the island's owner just yet. "The big question—where is it?"

"Lady, we've already covered that," Rob Brown said. "Nobody who leaves ever knows where it is."

"How is that possible?" Alicia voiced her frustration.

"They transport you in the hull," Harrison said. "Takes days. No sunlight. No windows. Nothing except stale food, water and buckets. But —" he sipped at a beer "—the pay's good."

"Fuck," Alicia muttered. "What the hell do we do now?"

"I heard it's in the Pacific," Chris Brown spoke up, staring away from them out of a nearby window. "Some of the other guys can read constellations, you know? And the climate is right for the Pacific."

Dallas shifted his feet. "Well, that narrows it down to over one hundred and fifty million square kilometers," he said, "in the largest and deepest of the world's oceans."

The mercs went silent. Hayden saw they'd squeezed about as much out of them as they were going to get. To be fair, it had been a reasonable meeting. Maybe the warm Spanish weather helped calm the ego.

Kinimaka looked around at her. "What next?" he asked.

"We look again," she said, glad to see determination in the big man's eyes. They would never give up. She reached out and placed a hand on his arm. "We will find them, Mano."

Harrison was watching her. "You know somebody on the island?"

Hayden berated herself, but decided the truth couldn't

hurt. "Four friends," she said. "Sent there against their will. We're trying to rescue them."

"You don't stand a chance," Chris Brown said. "The docks are the only safe entry and heavily guarded."

"Then we'll use an un-safe entry," Dahl growled.

"But then you'll have to cross the entire island," Rob Brown said. "Past the four clans. You'll die."

"That sounds suspiciously like you know where we could land," Drake said.

"No, no. It's just words."

Hayden saw there would be no more information. The mercs had said their piece and were waiting to be paid. She motioned to Kinimaka, who pulled out a thick wad and threw it onto the table.

The team retreated, heading for the door. Hayden opened it first and let everyone else through. Her eyes met those of the four mercs one last time but saw no compassion there, nothing other than severity.

Outside, the hot weather swathed them like a thick blanket. Molokai led the way back to the main street, where the team gathered.

"The Pacific?" Dallas whispered. "What next?"

Kenzie, who had remained silent in the bar, spoke up now. "We could find more mercs."

"I can try," Kinimaka said. "But that was the only thread on the web. My guess is certain keywords like 'the devil' self-delete after a certain time has passed. I could be more forthcoming, more open, but that could be asking for big trouble."

"I like big trouble," Dahl said. "Let's do that. Now."

They shaped up to move off, but a voice stopped them.

"Wait. I can help."

Hayden turned to see the older merc, Ray Harrison, a

step behind. The smile on his face lifted her heart.

Harrison sent a shifty glance back toward the bar and then urged them to move away. "Hurry," he said. "I don't have long."

CHAPTER THREE

Alicia Myles followed Harrison and the others across a busy road onto Salou's sandy beach. A deep blue stretched across the horizon.

Harrison led them to a bar and grabbed a seat. "Mai Tai," he told the waitress. "Two umbrellas."

Alicia settled in next to him. The others stood or sat around, ordering bottled water. The yellow beach before them was strewn with deck chairs and untidy sun worshippers, their belongings cast over wide areas. It was a long time since Alicia had sat on a beach, watching the sea. She couldn't even remember how that felt—the sense that everything was okay with the world, that nothing bad would ever happen, that nothing she could see or passed in the street would harm her.

She looked away from the horizon, away from the unknown adventures that it might contain. "Ray, was it?" she asked. "Tell us what you know."

"I know a guy." Harrison paused to sip his Mai Tai, smacking his lips afterward. "Wow, that's good. Yeah, so I know a guy. He was injured on the island."

"And why do we need to talk to him?" Dahl asked.

"Listen . . . you people can't land on Devil's Island and expect to survive more than a day without the knowledge this man can give you. Please believe me. I see you . . . I see you all. I get that you're experienced, smart, at the top of your game . . ."

Alicia patted Kinimaka's arm. "Don't worry, Mano. He'll get to your specialty in a minute."

Harrison hadn't stopped talking. ". . . your group is a good size to infiltrate and survive the island. But my friend—he survived that place for ten years. He lived with the Marauders as a spy and then at the castle. He saved my life once or twice down the years. The only time I reciprocated was when he broke his leg on the island. The Devil was ready to throw him from a cliff. I said I'd take him away and make sure he stayed quiet." Harrison spread his arms. "Which I did."

"Why would you want to help us?" Alicia asked. "Your friends don't seem overly arsed."

"Truthfully," Harrison said, "they told you everything they know. But if you really have friends trapped in that place . . ." He shuddered. "There are a thousand ways to die, and none of them pleasant."

"Would your friend have a map?" Hayden asked.

"He has everything. Like I said, he lived with the Marauders so mapped every inch of the island. And then he lived at the castle. He's the only man alive that will be willing to help you and, well . . . he needs money to stay off the grid."

"And why do you want to help us?" Drake asked.

"The man they call the Devil is . . . horribly, horribly evil. He lacks all conscience and has no morality. There are some men that shouldn't be allowed to exist on this earth—no matter the cost—and he ranks near the top of that list. Also, I value friendship." He shrugged. "I wouldn't wish your friends the same fate that I've seen others succumb to."

"There are worse things than this Devil," Dahl said softly. "We have seen many of them."

Harrison nodded. "Some are on this very island," he said. "Including the lava pits. The caves." He turned away. "You have no idea of evil, my friend. No clue. Not until you see the . . . things . . . he genetically modified."

Alicia repressed a shiver. "What the fuck are you talking about?"

"I can't speak of it." Harrison's face had turned bleach white under the red-hot sun. "I can't even think about it."

"All right," Hayden stepped in, "this friend of yours. Can you call him? Tell him to expect us?"

"Yes, yes." Harrison fought to recover. "I'll do that. He's based in Kuala Lumpur. Can you make that today?"

Hayden frowned. "It's a twelve-hour flight minimum," she said. "I'd say that puts us at tomorrow morning."

"I'll tell him to expect you." He took a scrap of paper offered by Dahl and wrote down an address. "He likes code words too. Anything preferable?"

Alicia jumped in. "If you're not living on the edge . . . you're taking up too much space."

Harrison turned to her. "I like that. Okay, I'll make it happen."

The team rose and readied to leave. Alicia paused a moment and bent down to whisper in Harrison's ear.

"What's your friend's name?"

"Tolley," was the answer. "Mick Tolley."

Alicia used the long flight to review the events of the last few weeks. After plucking the weapons of the gods from the greedy hands of Tempest, they had spent a few balmy days in London, taking their time storing the weapons in a secure vault and enjoying some downtime. It had been a kind of bliss. A few days alone with Drake, followed by a team get-together and then more time alone. It reminded her of all that she was missing, made her wonder if their lives were on the right path.

But then Luka Kovalenko made his attack, and everything changed. Again. They would never be the same—not least because of the deaths of Lauren and Smyth. And now—when Kovalenko's initial attack had been thwarted—the President saved—they were still without Mai, Luther, Karin and Dino. Devil's Island didn't sound like a nice place, but Alicia would take it in her stride.

Could she and Drake ever find a true, peaceful happiness?

We have to make changes. But it could be done. She saw the same question carved into Hayden's face now that she'd regained her true love. For Mano, that love had always been there. She knew Dahl and Johanna needed time to sit down and face their issues head on. She saw Kenzie still clinging to hope that the Swede might propose a future with her. Life had pounded them all to a pulp, forcing these emotions upon them but giving them no way to properly experience them.

Alicia craved a future with Drake now more than ever. She wondered how Mai and Luther would turn out. The opportunities were endless. And then there was Chika Kitano and Dai Hibiki, and Grace. What came next for them?

I stopped running for Drake. It changed my world. I found other ways to cope. The past is in the past and I won't allow it to destroy my future.

Drake, at her side throughout the flight, said very little. Maybe he too was working through some issues. *And,* Alicia thought proudly, *these are issues we can work together. Not alone. We're a family and we'll support each other through it all.*

The thought lifted her spirits so much so that she turned to the Yorkshireman. "Wanna earn your mile-high badge?"

Drake grunted. "Here? I think the others might object. Maybe not Kenzie but—"

"There's a bathroom, idiot."

"Wait a minute." Drake turned his head to look at her. "The question implies that you've already earned yours."

Alicia winced guiltily. "Ah . . ."

"And what makes you think I haven't earned mine?"

Alicia's eyed widened. "Have you?"

Drake leaned in, whispering. "That's for me to know and you to wonder about, love."

"Don't you want to know if I've earned mine?"

"Alicia," Drake patted her knee, "I've reconsidered, and the only question I now have is—how many times?"

She laughed, and they fell into silence again. It gave her time to assimilate up-to-date thoughts into deliberations over a new life, and what might come next. If the past had been about chasing horizons and the creed one life, live it; the new one was a little slower, a lot better, and infinitely scarier.

When you were running, seeking constant change, basing your life on what happened now and what came around the corner next, then the future wasn't important. It didn't matter if you lived or died mostly because . . . you had nobody who counted on you and nothing to lose.

But when you started thinking about a future, hundreds of issues raised prickly, inquisitive heads . . . there was mortality for a starter, she thought. She'd never imagined wanting to live into middle-age. There was fighting for the people who loved you, and never letting them down. Steering younger ones to make the right choices.

Staying put to stare a problem down the throat.

Alicia thought about responsibility and sighed. It was a hell of a lot harder than fighting a battle.

They didn't get to see a whole lot of Kuala Lumpur—or KL, as Hayden called it. The airport was generic, similar to a thousand more around the world. Once in the city proper she stared out of the grimy windows of their taxi as they were driven down a narrow road with market stalls to both sides, constantly slowing and often stopped by the flow of locals.

"Hot out there," Dahl said from the far left of the car. Alicia didn't answer. She was thinking about Mai and the others, even now being thrown around some distant ocean or fighting for their lives on Devil's Island. The only good news was that the Pacific was in this general direction, so every mile they traveled narrowed the distance. But, even for her, that was a stretch.

To their right, the buildings and general skyline was dwarfed by the Petronas Twin Towers, a 451-meter-tall pair of glass- and steel-clad skyscrapers and once the tallest building in the world. With the skies just starting to darken it shone like a beacon of wealth over all those that struggled by below.

Alicia looked away, keeping her eyes focused on the windshield. Soon, they pulled over and stopped behind the other taxi, idling in the street. The pedestrian flow parted around them as if they weren't there.

"Here," their driver said in English, pointing out of his window. "There."

Hayden thanked and paid him. The team met before a two-story, clapboard building, just another façade in a long, almost endless row. There was a door on the ground floor and a staircase to the right that led to a door on the next one. Hayden led them toward the staircase.

"Harrison should have called ahead," she reminded them. "But be prepared."

It went without saying. Sometimes Alicia wondered if Hayden spoke the obvious just to remind herself she was their leader but, hey, they were all happy with that scenario, so why speak out? It was loud out here, with heated conversations, the movement of people, and the expectant calls of street vendors all vying for supremacy.

Kinimaka climbed the stairs first, the others wincing as the wooden steps groaned with his passing, and hammered at the door.

Seconds later, it opened. Alicia saw a man that looked to be in his fifties but was probably younger, with a thick beard and a lustrous head of hair. He squinted at them as if his eyesight had recently failed, or perhaps he'd lost his glasses.

"Are you Mick Tolley?" Kinimaka asked.

"I might be," he responded. "Who are you?"

Alicia stepped forward. "If you're not living on the edge," she said. "You're taking up too much space. Let us in."

"There's a lot of you," he croaked. "Harrison didn't say there'd be a lot of you."

Kinimaka hesitated. Hayden moved to his side. "Would you prefer if just a few of us entered?"

"No, no," the man moved inside. "Get yourselves in here. Just don't expect it to be comfortable."

Alicia entered fifth in line and felt a little sympathy for the guy. You'd be hard pressed to swing a bag of shopping around. Tolley perched himself on a stool whilst Hayden and Kinimaka got the only couch. Everyone else either looked for a wall to lean against or stood in the middle of the room.

"Thanks for agreeing to see us," Hayden said. "It can't be easy—hiding from a man like the Devil."

Tolley scratched his beard. "What do you know of him?"

"Honestly, not much. Only that he's a scary guy without morals and that he likes to inflict pain."

Tolley sat back and reached for a half-eaten sandwich. The team waited for him to finish his bite. "I'm a thriller writer," he said. "On and off, but even I wouldn't dare to imagine—or recreate—the atrocities this monster has committed. I knew nothing of them when—as a seasoned merc—I first went to the island. Me and a dozen others. We thought we'd seen it all, heard everything. We were so wrong."

He paused to swig from a bottle of water. "The things we found on that island, the stories we heard . . . it scared us. Yeah, all of us. Grown men shivering in the night. You must understand the difference in mercs to accept that—there's your steady, dependable mercenary and then there's your military trained psychopath. Luckily, I rolled with a group of the former."

Hayden leaned forward, eyes intent. Kinimaka voiced the question in her eyes.

"What the hell did you find on that island?"

CHAPTER FOUR

Tolley tried to hide his fear. "Let me start with the Devil. He runs the island. Employs about a hundred mercs at a time and likes to keep them there. The smaller the turnover, the quieter his secret island stays. The sea journey, in and out, is made without access to windows. He lives in a large castle. There are captives on the island that he uses as slaves."

"This man shouldn't be allowed to live," Dahl muttered.

"You think that's the worst of it? Not even close. The Devil earned his name through thirty years of unique, bespoke murder. The darkest, most atrocious murders ever carried out. Say you want a family or board member killed, but it has to look like an accident. The Devil is the man you call. He's initiated riots that killed hundreds, local wars, traffic pile-ups, gang violence, terrorist attacks so that, each time, he could kill one single person."

Alicia struggled to get her head around that. "Is that even possible? Surely someone would know."

"They may suspect." Tolley shrugged. "The authorities, I mean. But they can't prove it. And would they confirm the existence of this monster to the general population, or would they say the plane that went down was destroyed by another nation? Or a pilot committing suicide? Or that a shooting was initiated by a crazed gunman unpopular in his youth? What do you think?"

"Do they know who he is?"

"They've never even seen his face. He visits the scene just

once. He monitors everything remotely; employs a small team he trusts to offer up scenarios. And when he's ready he initiates the plan, whether that be stoking the locals, killing a key gang member, infiltrating an airline or simply organizing a car accident."

There was a long silence. Tolley finished his sandwich and drank more water. He didn't offer any of his supplies to the group and Alicia didn't blame him. There didn't seem to be much to go around.

After a while, Tolley himself broke the silence. "And now he has a new target," he said. "Someone he's working on right now."

Alicia wondered if it might be one of the SPEAR team, but that thought didn't make sense. They came under fire almost daily. It wouldn't require a cleverly engineered "accident" to kill them.

"What target?" Dahl asked.

"I don't know. But he's been planning it for almost two months now."

"Maybe we can ask him when we see him," Kenzie said. "That'd be nice."

Dallas smiled. "Again, I'm so in tune with your thinking."

"I have this." Tolley rose and crossed to a battered chest of drawers, taking out a thick sheet of paper. "It's a map of the island."

"Perfect." Drake took it and held it up. Alicia saw a ragged coastline, border markings and other features clearly indicated.

"It's as well-defined as I can make it," Tolley said. "Some of the topography may be off—I recalled part of it from hearsay—but I believe it's pretty accurate."

"Thank you," Hayden said. "It could save our lives."

"You'll need more than a map. You have four clans to get

past, and I'd advise the quiet approach. You have the mountain. The genetic experiments. And then the castle itself and a hundred mercs before you even reach the Devil. Or your friends."

Alicia pricked her ears up at that. "What do you know?"

"Right." Tolley looked at the floor for a moment. "This is where I start risking my life. You must promise me you will kill the Devil. I mean wipe that bastard from the face of the earth. I've researched you—Team SPEAR. I know you're good. I know about your successes. I'm risking everything on you."

"It won't be a doddle, pal," Drake told him. "But we'll do our very best to take the wanker out."

Tolley smiled faintly. "Thanks . . . I think. I escaped the island due to injury. My team didn't. They were either killed there with the clan infighting or persuaded to see the Devil's view of life, losing their humanity. My mission has always been to avenge those good men. To that end . . . I have a friend on the island."

Alicia's spirits rose. "Finally, some good news."

"He's in deep," Tolley admitted. "Hard to contact. And it's beyond risky. Honestly, we were at a dead end before you guys showed up."

"Tell us what he's told you," Hayden said.

"Well, your nemesis—Luka Kovalenko—is on the island. Went there right after leaving Paris. He believes the Devil works for him but . . ." Tolley grimaced. "I doubt that very much. Anyway, Mai Kitano and the other three will be in the so-called Devil's Catacombs. They're here." He stepped across the room and tapped the map in Drake's hands. "That's the mountain and beneath it are the catacombs. There are exits here . . . and here. Notice it's just north of the castle and the dock area which is good, but it's also where the genetics live."

"These catacombs," Hayden said. "Are they a prison area?"

"No. I didn't visit them but heard a lot of whispers. It's more like . . . a proving ground. Only the strongest survive. Many die there, or so I'm told. The Devil's Catacombs is a fitting title."

Dahl walked over to Tolley. "Harrison told us we couldn't land at the docks," he said. "Too dangerous. Is there anywhere else we might land?"

Tolley nodded. "Here." He indicated a feature of coastline that looked like a ragged hook. "If you go ashore inside that curved headland you'll be sheltered from prying eyes and the worst of the elements, and the sea. It's a tough climb there, the cliffs are steep, but I'm guessing you've negotiated worse?"

Dahl grunted. "In the Swedish Special Forces, we climb cliffs for breakfast."

Drake stared at him, ready to tender the old Yorkshire wit, but Dallas beat him to it. "In SWAT we climb out of our SUVs into a local Denny's. I think I prefer that."

Alicia laughed, surprised the newcomer had once been a member of SWAT never mind confident enough to rib the Mad Swede. Both Drake and Dahl gave him an evaluating stare.

Tolley continued, "You'll have to negotiate the clans, the cliffs, the forests, the wild animals. The worst gang is called the Scavengers, but they're on the south-east side and might not even bother you. You head north, and then east." Again he indicated their journey on the map. "I'd come up to the northwest of the castle and find your friends from the top of the mountain."

"You mentioned . . . genetics?" Kenzie asked.

"An unknown quantity," Tolley admitted. "The Devil

spent a decade drafting in the best scientists, experimenting with animal DNA and mind control, but ultimately failed. Most of the test subjects died I think, but some . . . escaped . . . and roam those mountains to this day."

Alicia wanted to hear more—she'd never had much charity for scary or poisonous beasts—but Hayden checked her watch. "We need to move," she said, withdrawing a wad of cash from her pocket. "Can you tell us anything else?"

"My friend. Look after him. His name is Grant Hawkins. Oh, and take a drone with you. It'll help to scan the surrounding terrain and warn of any dangers."

Alicia thought that a great idea. "Let me ask you this," she said. "If everyone that visits the island doesn't know where it is . . . how can you?"

Tolley smiled broadly for the first time. "I'm old school," he said. "I don't rely on this new techno shit. Sat-nav. GPRS and the like. I can locate myself anywhere on the planet just by using the stars."

"I thought that might be it," Dahl said.

"Even the Devil can't hide the stars," Tolley said. "Let me give you the coordinates."

Ten minutes later they were gone, driving through the back streets of Kuala Lumpur once again. Full night had fallen and the streets, if anything, were even busier. Alicia saw every manner of trader she could think of through the car windows—and every type of consumer.

The last step of their journey to Devil's Island was a quick one. A final stop at a local CIA site to tool up, to pack and holster every weapon they could think of. Entire arsenals. Every gun and bullet and rocket launcher. Every strip of ammo, knives and grenades. They backed it up with the newest tech, the best gadgets. They attached some waterproof sheeting to the map and grabbed two state-of-the-art drones. In the end, they almost cleared the local armory out.

"We ready to go get our friends?" Hayden asked.

"Ready for war," Drake said.

"About bloody time," Alicia muttered.

"My last job," Kenzie said. "With all of you."

"Don't decide before Mai and the others are safe," Hayden said, "and you've heard what I have to say."

"Can't promise anything."

"I'm not asking you to."

"You guys gonna stand there gassing?" Molokai asked, his voice like low thunder. "Or are we gonna get my brother back?"

Alicia looked around at them, fully loaded and prepared to bring war to this lonely, deadly Pacific island.

"I think the Devil just met his match."

They moved out.

CHAPTER FIVE

Luka Kovalenko stared out the window of his room inside the Devil's mysterious castle, reflecting on recent events and looking forward to the next stages. The attack on the President and his family had failed and would have to be shelved—for now. No matter, it had paved the way for future plans and helped bring at least two SPEAR team members to this island. Soon, it would bring the entire team. Kovalenko wished he could stay—and watch the deaths of the traitorous Karin Blake along with the demise of Matt Drake, Alicia Myles and the others—but the failure with the President and the loss of Topaz had impacted his plans. He needed to recruit a new bodyguard first, and then a thinker to replace Andrei. The criminal underworld would know he'd lost his two best assets and would be . . . wondering.

He needed to respond to that with a harsh show of force.

The Blood King was here to stay. First, he'd prove it to them and then he'd make them enlist in his ever-growing army.

Thoughts of the future brought him back to the present. This was where it would start. His room was positioned on the eastern side of the castle, his window overlooking a courtyard, the beach and the docks. He could see his superyacht, moored beyond the shallows. A flurry of activity across the docks. Mercenaries stalking this way and that, carrying boxes or herding prisoners. Delivering supplies. This island had been the best place in the world to spend a few quiet days whilst the authorities chased down every nugget of information, wasting resources as they searched for him. Kovalenko had rested here in luxury whilst they searched the lowest rat holes of Eastern Europe and Russia itself.

And so, to the next part of his extensive plan. A discreet knock on the door interrupted his train of thought, which vexed him. "Yes?"

A slave shuffled in with the meal he'd ordered. Kovalenko sprang over to punch the hapless individual for ruining his thought process. There was no struggle, no sound, not even the slightest attempt to put up a defense. Kovalenko liked that. He lashed out again and again, making the slave bleed, making him crumple to the floor. He laughed. *How much damage can I do for free?*

At first the idea excited him, but then on reflection, it pained him. There was an unspoken rule on this island. The Devil owned it. Kovalenko preferred to believe that wasn't the case, and that the Devil worked for him.

But right now, in this moment, it was a belief he couldn't physically test.

Wait. It will all come to you.

His mantra for years, ever since his father was murdered at the hands of the SPEAR team. Luka had turned waiting into an art form.

He kicked the slave out of his room, then settled at the table to start on a plate of green olives and sundried tomatoes. Where had his thoughts been when the stupid slave knocked? It didn't take more than a moment to recall.

What comes next?

Well, SPEAR would immolate right here. Either that or be killed by warring gangs, genetic monsters or mercenaries. It all sounded good to him. Devil's Island was quite probably the most dangerous place on earth—especially when Kovalenko initiated his next step.

He'd considered it long and hard. Topaz and, in particular, Andrei had warned against it. But they were dead. They hadn't wanted to infuriate the Devil by taking this next step. Kovalenko didn't care. They'd reminded him of what the man did for a living, of where his legend had been created. Kovalenko no longer cared. Legends were made to be torn down. Wasn't his father the embodiment of that?

He hated the Devil and all his machinations.

But there were other things on this island that Kovalenko wanted to hide. Far worse things than the Devil himself.

His cell beeped. Kovalenko answered immediately, knowing that for the next step to succeed timing was of the essence. "Hello?"

"Sir, we are ready to sail at a moment's notice."

"You have every supply I noted?"

"Yes, sir."

"That is good." Kovalenko eyed his main course with some regret. It looked delicious. But still . . . there was always the yacht and its facilities.

"Prepare red wine poached halibut with bacon and garlic toasts. I want it ready for our departure in, say, twenty minutes."

"I will see to that, sir."

Kovalenko ended the call. Happy that his dining plans were in order, he turned his thoughts to the murder of several hundred people and, on the back of that, several thousand more.

The plutonium had been stolen from an abandoned Soviet cold war facility decades ago. It had resided in Russia and then Kazakhstan for years, awaiting the arrival of men with the skills to enhance its potential. It had been forgotten about, transported openly on trucks, taken to Afghanistan only five years ago. As time passed technological advances increased. Things could be done with the plutonium now that could not be done back then. It had remained stable. Those that carried it did not want repercussions. It had also remained secret . . . almost.

Kovalenko heard of it through Andrei. Of course. *Most of my insider knowledge and connections came from Andrei. His loss is irreplaceable.* It took months, but finally they had tracked the plutonium down to a nasty part of Chechnya near the border of Azerbaijan. Kovalenko had sent men to extract it with extreme prejudice and—days later—had been the proud owner of a football-sized piece of plutonium. The next step was finding scientists that knew what to do with it and then locating a place to store it.

And then work began on it. Turning it into something Kovalenko was proud of.

Striking a deal with the Devil, Kovalenko stored it on the island. He sent scientists there to transform it. The Devil had balked at first but was then offered a lot of money. Of course, it was Andrei that found out the Devil was struggling to fund his mercenary army, defend his castle and buy supplies. Everything fitted perfectly.

The plutonium had been turned into a weapon. No, that's incorrect. It had been made into twenty weapons. Each one a mini nuclear bomb with a plutonium core, carefully fashioned. Each one less than a quarter of a megaton. These plutonium cores had been inserted into small warheads with enough explosive charge to detonate them.

Nineteen were now stored upon the Blood King's superyacht.

And the twentieth?

Kovalenko laughed as he finished off the olives and stood up. He couldn't stop a rush of euphoria. He didn't flinch when his left foot slipped in blood left by the careless slave he'd beaten. He wiped his sole on a rug and ambled back to the window.

Deep below him, in the foundations of the castle, the twentieth plutonium core waited.

He wanted Devil's Island gone. Obliterated. He wanted the clans that roamed it gone. He wanted the Devil and the SPEAR team gone. But most of all he wanted to hide what had been done here. He wanted to cover up the fact that six of Eastern Europe's foremost nuclear scientists had been forced to create twenty low-yield nuclear weapons.

He would do that by detonating one of them.

Looking over the mass of activity at the docks, thinking about the tall building behind his—the so-called keep where the Devil lived—Luka Kovalenko reveled in pulling out his cellphone and typing in a number.

A signal was sent to the bomb, arming it. The countdown began.

One down, he thought. Nineteen more to go.

But where should he send the others?

The next part of his plan beckoned.

CHAPTER SIX

Mai Kitano sat upright against the cave wall, rubbing at any bruise she could reach. Her head still reeled from the ocean voyage. The hard ground beneath her seemed to move with a gentle roll. She closed her eyes, trying to stop the sensation but that just made it worse. Feeling nauseous, she took a deep breath and opened them again, trying to focus.

Where the hell were they?

The nightmare journey had ended just a few hours ago. The cargo ship dropped anchor and drifted to a stop—not that it had been going particularly fast in the first place. Luther had assumed they'd be a few miles off shore, in deep water.

It took almost an hour for their door to be opened and natural sunlight to flood in. For the first time in what felt like months they were led outside, bathed in warmth, their eyes closed to shield them from this new assault on the senses. From that point their guards bullied, prodded and shoved them across the ship's deck and deposited them in a large dinghy.

When Mai was able she evaluated their guards. Some stood close enough to tackle, but many more watched from the ship, some on deck and others up high. All carried automatic weapons, and she counted at least fifty. When her eyes caught Luther's, he shook his head ever so slightly.

"Later," he muttered.

She understood. He wanted to get the hell off this ship and onto dry, firm land as much as she did. The dinghy smashed them through wave after wave as it headed for a sandy shore. Mai hung on, feeling battered, her head whirling. She saw both Dino and Karin throw up over the side, weak from endless days of sailing coupled with meagre food and their living quarters. It was something Mai just wanted to forget.

The dinghy made a hard landing on the beach. Guards surrounded them. To the left, Mai saw a wide, asphalted path at the end of a nearby jetty, leading straight to a fenced compound. The path was full of mercenaries wearing fatigues and T-shirts, holding their weapons at ease. Many were joking among themselves as they fetched and carried.

The compound walls were manned by more soldiers. Beyond that she saw several buildings surrounded by a castle wall, the central tower standing higher than all the others. It was a hot day, humid. Already, she was sweating. Mai welcomed it, hoping the heat might squeeze out some of the toxins that had collected inside her body over the last few days. But she needed water. Lots of it.

Instead, they were dragged along the beach, past the noisy compound, toward a large, craggy mountain. Here, Mai caught a glimpse of a smaller compound sitting against the base of the towering rock face; this one separated into cell-like cages. Faces were pressed up against the bars, staring out at the passersby with a desolate lifelessness.

"You have prisoners here?" she asked. "Is that where you're taking us?"

The only answer was a rifle butt to the kidneys. Mai gasped and staggered. Luther kept her from falling, receiving similar treatment for his actions.

They did not stop. Mai was no stranger to adversity—all her life had been spent fighting one enemy or another. From the Ninja clan that her parents sold her to and its enigmatic but appalling leader, from Yakuza far and wide, and a hundred other enemies, Mai Kitano had faced almost every form of hardship on the planet.

And she had faced all of it down.

It molded her. It forged the warrior that now shone forth. But she never forgot where she came from—two loving parents forced through poverty and the twisted words of a conman to give her away. And she never forgot her sister and friends.

Mai had found her parents. She had seen Chika discover love with an old friend of hers. And she had fought battles in Japan to save Grace, also taken by the Ninja clan but now living the best life that she could. Weeks ago, Mai had come to the conclusion that she wanted to share her life with someone. Some time ago, it would have been Matt Drake—but that chance was gone, and she didn't begrudge it. She'd realized that the door was open to play the field, to test the waters.

Of course, then she met Luther. The issue with the American was her own misgivings. Luther was the first man she'd liked since Drake—was she rushing in? Was she too needy? Was she settling when she could speculate?

Before any of these questions could be answered, the Blood King came along and wrecked everything. Now, oddly, she was glad it was Luther who'd been kidnapped with her. She'd see him for the kind of man he was.

The beach ended where impassable rocks began. Their captors—eight in total—dragged them through the uneven stones with the high cliff face to their left, the crashing waves to their right. It was a narrow path. When Mai turned, she saw another group following them, this group dressed differently to the regular mercs and eighteen strong. She didn't have long to look but thought there might be civilians among them.

She was at the head of their group, hands tied behind her back, Luther a step behind. Karin and Dino were further back, heads low, walking as if they were already defeated. Mai had to make herself remember that those two hadn't faced the life challenges that she had. They weren't as seasoned.

She trudged on, skin alight where the sun beat down on it, face and hair sprayed by sea foam. Ever since she left the ship she'd been trying to snag a glance at a merc's watch. She knew it was early morning, but wanted an exact time. Now she saw that it was a little after 5 a.m. Steadily, they left the compound and its buildings and cages behind and circumvented the mountain. Its rock face towered over them. Sometime later they stopped and were ushered into a craggy cave entrance. Mai ducked her head to enter.

Down and down for what seemed like an hour they trudged. The darkness was absolute, but the time gave Mai—and she hoped her companions—time to shed the debilitating miasma that the voyage had injected her with. The way was lit by flickering torches set into the rock walls at varying intervals.

At last, they came to a wide, high, well-lit cave. Their captors told them to sit in a corner and listen. All four were handed a bottle of water and then randomly kicked. Mai couldn't shuffle away from the blows in the tight space, but held on to her bottle and took it. Pain flared from her shin, her thigh. Luther sat and accepted it, stoic faced. Karin and Dino tried to crawl away, but the aggressors only followed and made their blows harder.

Now, Mai nursed her bruises and watched as their captors gave way to the other eighteen men she'd seen following. Everyone fitted inside the cave. Most of the men rested on their haunches, faces glowing eerily in the flickering light as they were thrown into amber relief and then shadow. Their eyes didn't change though, Mai noticed; they glinted with an unyielding malice.

A man that she assumed was their leader stepped forward. He stood in front of them for a minute, assessing their situation, his mouth twisted into a harsh smile. From a sheath on his right hip he withdrew a knife.

"I'm Valance," he said, his black eyes merciless, his face harsh. "You're inside a very large cave system. Can you hear that?"

Mai, surprised, cocked her head to the left. She'd been too focused on her situation to think about anything else until now but there . . . very faint . . . was a deep rumbling sound.

"Volcano," Valance said. "Oh, don't worry. It's not active, but it's damn close. It's not going to erupt any time soon. It's never properly erupted. But you will find on your way through these tunnels that some of those old tubes still carry molten lava."

Mai finished off her bottle of water, saying nothing.

"There's one way out of this cave system." He pointed to a tunnel that vanished deeper into the mountain. "Through there. You four will run. We will track you and then kill you. I'll give you a five-minute head start."

He paused, letting it sink in. Mai couldn't help but glance at Luther and then look over at Karin and Dino. Everyone understood; they just didn't know why.

"You brought us all this way just to hunt us?" Mai said. "There are caves in Europe too. Even the odd volcano."

"Not our choice." Valance shrugged. "That decision was made between the Blood King and the Devil. Quite a pair, those two. Nutty as a squirrel's birthday cake and as deadly as Sarin. But hey, as soon as we made the right financial offer they were hugely accommodating. Can't say fairer than that."

"Financial offer?" Mai shook her head, not understanding.

Valance ran the blade of his knife over rock, sharpening its edge. "It's a game. A competition. Fourteen mercenaries and four civilians against the great Mai Kitano and Luther . . ." He paused, thinking. "Do you even have a second name, bro?"

"Fuck you."

"Really? I bet that gives you fond memories of your school days. So . . . we get you two and also the two rookies to play with." He laughed at Karin and Dino. "We will have the guns, but I will allow you knives and a pack of supplies. I'll also let you keep the flak jackets you rolled in with. We could be down here for some time. The passage there—" he nodded toward it "—meanders for miles. It has junctions, dead ends, death traps. We have added several surprises of our own . . ." The assemblage giggled. "But eventually it does emerge at the top of the mountain. If you can make it that far. By that time though . . . you or all of us will be dead."

"You paid the Devil for this?" Mai hissed. "You're all mad."

"Yeah, yeah, we sold our souls. When we catch you we will kill you. That's all you really need to know."

"Who are these four civilians?" Karin asked. "Have you abducted and forced them too?"

Valance laughed. "You're kidding me, right? They're the reason we're all here. No, they're four rich white hunters. They've paid for the privilege to hunt you, with us watching their backs."

In a terrible way, it made sense. Mai grimaced and then

caught Valance's eye. "You know you're all gonna die, don't you?"

The man continued scraping his knife. "I would expect nothing less from you." He made a quick signal and a backpack was thrown at Mai's feet. Then Valance twirled his finger at the captives, asking them to turn around.

"Guns," he said.

Fourteen mercs came forward, their weapons aimed.

"When I cut you free, don't attack," he said. "I want to kill you in the tunnels where it's more of a fair fight, not here." He snipped their bonds.

Mai rubbed her wrists and reached for the backpack, checking its contents. There was more water, energy bars, a first-aid kit, and several other items she didn't have time to check. Without asking she passed the others an energy bar and tucked into hers. She drank more water.

Valance tapped a rock with his knife. "Ready?"

His men threw them large military blades with serrated edges along the top. To their credit, these were serious weapons.

"One last thing," Valance said, looking more serious. "This island blows to kingdom come in twenty-four hours." He checked his watch. "Mark."

Everyone pressed a button on their watches.

"I'd say a distance of three miles would be adequate," he went on. "If you have the energy left to swim that far."

Valance laughed. His men smiled. The civilians with their large guns stared at Mai with an intense hatred.

"Best get moving," Valance said. "Your time starts now."

CHAPTER SEVEN

The small jet flew out of thick cloud and dipped toward the sea. Drake and the others were ready to jump. It was a military jet, equipped with a special cargo hold from which they could perform a low altitude parachute jump.

When the doors opened the team leaped out. Drake plummeted hard toward the roiling sea, pulled at his ripcord and, as always, felt a moment's relief when it unraveled without a hitch. The whole team sounded off that all was okay. Eight-strong, they flew at the bright blue seas, cutting away from their chutes at the last minute. They sliced into the ocean feet first, waiting for the momentum to slow before kicking their legs and heading back up to the surface.

Then they bobbed for a while, scouting the coast.

Ahead, nothing moved. Drake saw the hook of land that Hawkins had recommended. It took some effort with the weight they carried, but he trod water, scanning the high cliffs rising above. Nothing stirred in the early morning.

"Let's go."

They struck out at a steady pace. Every member of the team was fully loaded, packing enough weapons and ammo to end a war. Other supplies were strapped to their backs, and items for day and night work. Hopefully, they hadn't left anything to chance.

Drake reached the headland first and swam around it into a narrow cove that was sheltered from the sea. The water was shallower here and he found himself wading forward, still studying the cliff face ahead. With this being the western side of the island and the cliffs rising so high it was still gloomy and cold, everything wrapped with the last vestiges of shadow.

Drake waded onto a beach and removed his face mask. It shouldn't be needed again. An amphibian aircraft was on standby from the nearest island and there were many boats at anchor near the castle that they might be able to utilize.

From out of nowhere, a figure appeared to his left, rising and attacking in one swift move. Drake was barely able to catch a downward swing on the material of his heavy jacket, deflecting the huge knife blade away from his skin. He was vaguely aware of other bodies attacking from left and right, emerging from the waves.

What the hell were they doing—fishing?

Struggling in the undertow, he staggered to the right. The attacker was on him in a second. Drake twisted his upper body, throwing the man off. Water splashed. Heavy waves crashed over them. He caught his first real glimpse of his adversary as they faced off. The man had a thick head of hair that hung in limp hanks, brown eyes and a beard. Sores pitted the side of his mouth and nose. Even from here Drake could tell he was largely unwashed.

The knife thrust forward. Drake was ready now, twisting and catching the wrist above the handle. He jerked hard, snapping bone. The man grunted. The knife fell into the waves. Drake pressed his advantage, but another breaker rolled past and forced him sideways. The man disappeared momentarily, then came up spluttering.

Drake righted himself and glanced toward the deeper ocean. The waves would never stop coming but he had a short window now. He leapt, forcing his enemy's head down and removing his own knife from its sheath around his waist. Quickly, he stabbed three times, felt the life force leave his aggressor, and let the body float.

Drake turned. Finally, he could see what else was going on. There were only two other attackers. It was the surprise of their assault that had upset the team. But only momentarily. Alicia and Molokai were dispatching one man whilst Dahl held another under the rushing water, foam spinning in a little whirlpool where his arm breached the waves. The next large wave broke over them. Drake fell to his knees, spluttering. When he looked up, Dahl was already stalking to shore, having finished with his man. The rest of the SPEAR team followed.

"I've had better welcomes," Alicia gasped, catching her breath.

"I'm surprised," Kenzie said. "You being you."

"Piss off, I didn't see you helping."

"I knew Molokai could handle it."

"I was helping Molokai."

"Yeah, but despite that I knew he could still handle it."

Drake tuned them out as he caught his breath and stared up at the black craggy cliff face before them.

"Not my forte," Kinimaka grunted from behind. "If men were meant to climb mountains they'd have a spring-loaded cams instead of fingers."

"Hawaiian proverb?" Hayden asked.

"My proverb."

"One brisk climb and we're up," Dahl said. "From the terrain image we saw before we jumped, I think this range drops into a small valley, and then we have another shorter range to cross before it all evens out into valleys and fields."

"Don't forget the Marauders," Kenzie said, squeezing salt water out of her hair. "The mountains are their territory."

Drake was happy they'd been given some extra peace of

mind with the satellite image. "Everything we saw relates to the map Hawkins gave us," he said. "It's accurate. We can explore with confidence."

By now the others had joined them. Molokai and Alicia came last, the blonde having trouble with her flippers and cursing them to hell and back.

"Not like you to take your time shedding clothes," Drake noted.

"That's because, in the bedroom, I'm not used to taking off fucking flippers."

"Well, maybe you can work on that." He grinned and turned away.

Dahl had already spied the easiest and safest route up the cliff. "See." He traced it in the air with his finger. "It's not direct but there are ledges and resting points. Plenty of crevices. Follow me."

They fell into line as Dahl approached the base. At that moment a loud crack sounded, and a bullet whizzed off the rock near his shoulder.

Drake fell to the floor, staring up into the rocks. The problem was they all looked the same—black granite. The briefest of movements allowed him to pinpoint their enemy.

"Two o clock," he said into the comms. "About fifty feet up."

"Why'd they only take a pot shot?" Dallas wondered.

"Sentries," Kenzie speculated. "In my experience they're always sluggish. They get used to nothing ever happening."

"Maybe . . ."

Drake raised his most accurate weapon, a fourth generation M16 that could be equipped with enough accessories to confuse even the most seasoned soldier. Drake's sported lasers and tactical lights and should be good for target practice.

He sighted in on the rocks where he'd seen movement. He didn't want to fire before a good opportunity arose. The others had hit the dirt around him. Dahl pressed himself against the rock face.

A head popped up, rifle following. Drake opened fire. He saw a gout of blood through the sights, and then the head fell away. It was followed by another. Bullets were loosed. They slammed into the sand and the rocks, fired without direction and seemingly in a panic. Drake thought he saw a radio antennae close to a man's left ear a moment before he opened fire.

"Good shot," Molokai said.

The second man flew back into the rock face before slithering out of his hidey hole and down the cliff. Dead, he fell in a jumbled mess, landing on the beach with a loud slap. Hayden dashed over to make sure the man was dead.

"Up," Dahl said.

Taking care, they started up the rock face. Handholds were good and plentiful so they didn't need to attach cams, but Dahl hammered several in anyway, to help those less experienced than him. With Molokai's help he threaded ropes between several of them so those below could match the leader's pace. Time was of the essence if they were to cross the island and save their friends.

Drake took it a step at a time, move by move. He tested every handhold, every surface. The last thing he wanted was to take a nose dive at one hundred feet, sandy surface or not.

They stopped momentarily to check on the men they'd killed, searching for a radio. Dahl didn't find one, but did come up with a cellphone.

"Interesting. There's electricity here. And not just at the castle."

He guessed it made sense. If the legends were true, the Devil had initially invited these men to live on the island. They would have sources of electricity, running water and other essential needs.

After a brief rest they continued up the rock face. Drake's gloves helped protect his fingers, but the strain grew. At his back he could sense and hear the sea, pounding relentlessly at the coastline; he could feel gusts of wind as they tried to pluck him off his narrow perch. But he could also feel a rising heat, the higher they climbed, a brightening of the day.

They were climbing into sunlight.

And onto Devil's Island.

CHAPTER EIGHT

Up and over the top, they went. Eight soldiers seeking to rescue their friends in one of the most inhospitable places on the planet. Drake went over third, trusting that Dahl's and Molokai's lack of warning was a good thing.

It was.

A flat surface extended to a boulder field ahead, beyond which Drake saw a wide stretch of rocky ground and then another set of cliffs. These towered above and would have to be climbed straight away. On the plus side, they looked as painless to navigate as the ones they'd just climbed.

Dahl and Molokai ranged out, heads down, checking the area. Drake waited until Hayden and Kinimaka joined him and then moved forward. A rising sun warmed both them and the landscape. It spread spectacularly across the eastern horizon, a layered bank of reds and yellows that slowly illuminated the land. Drake kept his eyes peeled to the scenery, checking for the slightest movement.

"Remember," Dahl said. "They're not soldiers, but they are hardened criminals, engaged in this kind of covert warfare for years. Don't underestimate them."

Drake checked the compass that was strapped to his right wrist. East was dead ahead.

"Don't be premature," Alicia whispered at his side. "We gotta climb those bastards yet." She pointed at the cliff face.

"I've never been premature in my life, Alicia. You should know that."

She looked at him. "Really? There was that one time in Casablanca . . ."

Drake shook his head quickly. "I've never been to Casablanca."

"That wasn't you? Oh, well, he looked like you."

Drake wasn't sure whether to be annoyed or grateful and decided not to respond. They were in the boulder field now and among good cover. The eight-strong team picked its way through the scattered stones, ranging to left and right, moving ahead with guns held ready. Barely a sound was made. Ahead, there was a slight gap in the cliff, a serrated, uneven hole through which they could see down to a small patch of the island beyond.

Drake saw a deep valley and a wide forest, more mountains and a winding river. Already, he could see different climate zones at work here, and wondered how many there might be on this small island. He knew the Big Island in Hawaii was spectacular in that the tiny lump of rock contained eight out of the world's thirteen climate zones, which meant you could experience the verdant fern forests of Puna, the rugged lava plains of Kona, the mists of Waimea Canyon and the snowy heights of Mauna Kea in a matter of hours. He could see pieces of that through the gap in the mountain. Recalling the map, he imagined the wilderness to the far southeast might be divided by a canyon and they already knew there was a stagnant volcano to the northeast.

"This place would make a pretty good tourist trap," he commented as they walked. "Once you've removed all the murderers and savages."

"And the Devil," Kenzie reminded him.

"Yeah, and a shitload of mercenaries," Alicia said.

"Is that the official term for a group of mercs?" Dallas asked. "I didn't know that."

Alicia looked over. "As soon as we get a spare minute, we

need to talk about you. We don't know you, and Kenzie here can't be trusted with her judgment."

"Okay—" Dallas started to agree.

"Me!" Kenzie hissed, her voice low. "You're not exactly renowned for making good choices, bitch."

"It's fine," Dallas interjected, trying to stem the altercation. "I get it. You're a world-class, tight-knit group, able, and forced to rely on one another to stay alive. I understand why you wouldn't trust a newcomer straight away."

"It's not just that," Drake said, thinking of those that were no longer here. "We don't want to get you killed, mate."

"You're with the bitch on this?" Kenzie drove her words at him.

"Let me ask you, how well do you know Dallas? He could be a spy. It's happened before."

Kenzie looked between Drake and Dallas, and then at Alicia. Disbelief then wariness entered her gaze. She was well aware of the Blood King's nefarious methods, his long-term plans, his ability to wait. A new light came into her eyes as she stared at Dallas.

"We could throw him off the next cliff if you like."

Alicia shifted around a rock. "Now you're talking."

Drake threw his arms around Dallas' shoulders. "They're joking," he said. "For now. You did show up at an opportune time and we really do need to have a chat, but let's wait until the days and nights are easier, hey mate?"

Dallas hadn't so much as batted an eyelid. "Fine with me."

"Good."

The boulder field fizzled out. Dahl and Molokai ranged further afield, circumventing the base of the cliff face ahead.

Hayden walked as close as she dared to the narrow gap that afforded them a glimpse of the island beyond.

"Across there, somewhere, is the castle," she said. "And the Devil. A shame we couldn't have parachuted in closer."

Kinimaka squinted through the gap. "Too much noise," he said. "We'd have alerted every savage on the island."

"I guess."

Drake came up to them. "Sorry, Mano, no matter how much you try, you're not gonna fit through there."

Kinimaka flexed his muscles. "No, but you might if I shove you hard enough."

They smiled. Hayden turned her gaze up about two hundred feet, studying the cliff face before them. "One more climb," she said. "I'm surprised we haven't encountered more sentries."

"Don't say that," Alicia joined them. "It's bad luck."

"How far to the castle?" Dallas asked.

"Map's not to scale," Dahl said, still scanning their surrounds. "From our brief look above, I'd say the journey from west to east will take several hours."

"Cheers," Drake grumbled. "A moment of pure clarity from the Great White Journey Guru."

"Assuming we don't run into any islanders," Dahl added. "Or don't decide to feed our Yorkshire terrier to them." He glared at Drake.

Hayden coughed, no doubt reminded of the slice of flesh she'd been forced to consume during their Peruvian escapade. Molokai returned to the group at that point.

"The cliffs are clear," he said. "And so are the surrounds. Perfect time to start up."

Drake took a moment to arrange his gear, thinking that his fingertips and toes hadn't recovered from the last climb yet. His knees were gashed, and his elbows strained. The upside was that the ascent hadn't taken too long and these cliffs were roughly the same height. They also appeared to offer more in the way of handholds and actual wide ledges where they might be able to gain several feet without having to cling to the rocks like monkeys.

All good.

The sun was climbing now, breaching the splash of gold that stretched across the eastern skies. It wouldn't be long before it began to beat down.

"Let's get this done," he said.

"And hope to God there's a decent coffee shop at the top," Alicia said.

The team moved out, following Dahl and Molokai. They stowed weapons and tugged on climbing gloves, took a last recce around the area, and focused on the cliff faces, ready to climb.

"Hardest part of the journey." Dahl grinned. "The rest will be as easy as tracking an Englishman through Stockholm."

Drake screwed his eyes shut and wondered if the "don't jinx it" term properly translated to Swedish. Either way, the spell had been cast.

CHAPTER NINE

Intent on climbing the rock face, the team reined in their surveillance, which contributed to the last-minute warning from Molokai that they were under attack.

Drake was moving between ledges, an easy task, but heard Molokai shout and immediately looked around. The movement overbalanced him and for one dreadful moment he was tilting over a hundred-foot drop, but then he reached out, grabbed rock and pulled himself back.

His eyes focused.

Climbing up from below were three men. Standing on the top of the cliff they'd originally climbed, probably two hundred feet apart now, were three more men. Four others stood in the boulder field below and, above, two more stared down. Drake thought they'd just arrived from different directions. It was the only explanation that made sense.

"Marauders," Hayden said over the comms. "This is their territory."

"Agreed," Dahl said. "Keep moving up."

Drake jumped to cover, landing on a ledge with a jagged, three-foot-high chunk of rock between him and the Marauders. He took another few seconds to see what kind of weapons they carried, but it was hard to make out at this distance.

"Rifles for sure," he said. "I can't tell if they're good quality though."

"One thing's certain," Dahl said. "Ours are better."

Holding on to the cliff with one hand and aiming his rifle with the other, the Swede loosed a quick volley at the climbers below. Bullets glanced off the rock face and zinged away.

Drake shook his head. "Bloody show off."

Molokai copied Dahl's example, but Drake wasn't the accomplished climber they both appeared to be. He ducked out, lined the men on the opposite cliff up in his sights and loosed four quick shots. Instantly, they split, leaping aside and rolling to the floor. He didn't think he'd hit anyone.

"Climb," Dahl urged.

The team reached for the handholds, dragging themselves up the rock face, finding a toe hold or a finger crevice, holding for a moment before lunging up to the next safe ledge. Drake was fifth in line with Alicia and Kenzie close by. Dallas was last. Gunfire rang out through the valley and bullets flew. Drake took a quick glance around, losing focus on the climb. Those coming up in their wake were about forty feet below but firing as they came. Rock climbing would come easy to them. The ones on the ground were chancing pot shots. Those on the opposite cliff were kneeling, placing rifles over their shoulders and taking aim.

"Cover!" he cried.

He hunched up, unable to find a safe ledge. Around him the others did the same. Bullets impacted close to Kenzie's head and to the right of Alicia's backpack. The sound of gunfire echoed between opposing cliff faces, rebounding and growing louder. More came.

Drake heaved himself up, one toe-hold to another and then launched his body at a ledge. It was wide, enabling him to roll onto it and into the cliff. He hit hard but safely. A bullet slammed into the rock where his body had just been. More shots rang out.

He rose to a kneeling position, gun nestled against his shoulder. Covering fire needed to be laid down. He alternated between all three enemy positions, giving them something to think about. In another minute, Alicia joined him and Kinimaka was firing from somewhere above.

They were about fifty feet from the cliff top.

Dahl and Molokai were keeping those above at bay. For a moment there was a standoff, but Drake knew they couldn't stay here. The Swede leaned out precariously, trying to improve his chances of a kill-shot, but almost overbalanced when a bullet fired from the opposite ridge shattered rocks to his left.

Dahl bellowed for better cover.

Kenzie and Dallas leapt and rolled to safety further along the same ledge as Drake and the others. Together, they all leaned over and loosed a deadly volley of hundreds of bullets that smashed down among the enemy. The mini-canyon vibrated with tremendous noise.

Drake was pleased to see men scattering and ducking for cover. He scanned the next fifty feet upward. "Watch my back!" he cried.

Leaping for a handhold, he brought his feet up fast and launched himself upward through the air. The gun swiped him about the face, but he ignored it. One more jump and he reached a higher ledge—eight feet closer to safety. Relying on Dahl and Molokai, he leaned out and aimed down, keeping the men below occupied.

Alicia and Hayden followed his ascent, landing half a minute later.

"Good move."

"There's another ledge ten feet above us. Same again?"

"Let's wait for Mano and the others first." Hayden glared straight down the craggy rock face. "The climbers are closing quite quickly."

Drake glanced down. They were only twenty feet below, ascending rapidly but shrewdly too, almost always hugging the rock, keeping it between them and enemy fire. Drake tried a couple of potshots, missed and almost got his own head blown off in the process.

"We'll deal with them in a minute."

Alicia and the others rolled over into relative safety, landing on the ledge and grabbing handholds to stay secure.

"Anyone tagged one of them yet?" she panted.

"Nope," Drake answered. "But on the plus side they haven't tagged any of us either."

"Well, I got shot during the last mission," Alicia said. "I'll take a pass on this one."

"I got shot twice on the last one," Drake pointed out. "No way am I catching a bullet this time."

Dahl's dry voice came over the comms. "That's because you're shit, mate."

Drake deigned to remain silent. They laid down fire as Dahl and Molokai climbed to the next ledge, and then looked ten more feet up.

"Ready?" Hayden asked.

Drake was. Taking a deep breath and steadying his weapons, he reached up for the first handhold but froze in shock when Dahl cried out, "Grenade!"

The word didn't compute. Up here? But he'd never question Dahl. Knowing the ledge was directly beneath him he folded, hitting the rock and covering up. An explosion battered his eardrums seconds later; shrapnel pinged against rocks, striking just over his head and against the short rock wall that protected them.

Drake glanced up in time to see one of the men above throw a second grenade into the air. This one fell fast. He ducked again, but the explosion occurred a few feet below them, shattering rock. Dahl and Molokai clung to their handholds as best they could.

Would they try another? Drake didn't think so. There was too much chance involved. They could kill their own climbing men. Moving fast, he took a quick recce below and across the gap. Nothing much had changed. Without pause and somewhat recklessly, he leapt for a handhold and pulled himself up to the next ledge. Now, he was only twenty feet from the top.

He paused, waiting. Alicia and Hayden started up, covered by Kinimaka. Kenzie and Dallas were further to the right, covering each other. He fired a burst at the ground, but it was far away now. He didn't expect to hit anyone. A savage gust of wind tore at his chest, almost physically moving him. He wiped sweat from his eyes.

Welcome to Devil's fucking Island, he thought.

All three men on the opposite cliff were firing. Drake ignored them. They were idiots thinking they could score a hit from that distance. Below, Alicia and Hayden grabbed handholds but then the enemy climbers appeared over the ledge, leaping up and dragging at the two women's backpacks to pull them off the cliff. Drake put his rifle to his shoulder, its sight to his right eye. Below, Alicia fell at the feet of her opponent; Hayden followed suit with hers.

Kinimaka had spun and was trying to draw a bead on the two enemy Marauders. Unable to get a clean shot, he holstered the weapon and pounded along the narrow ledge. Drake switched his vision between both women, waiting for a chance.

Alicia hit the ground hard, her breath stolen away. By the time she recovered, a boot was stamping on her face, drawing blood from her nose. She elbowed it away, reached for her gun, but then her opponent landed on her stomach, knees first, driving even more air out of her. Alicia raised her arms for cover. A knife flashed down, and glanced away from her wrist protection. The Marauder overbalanced. She heaved him to the right then launched her body straight at him, meeting him face to face for the first time.

A hardened merc. A warrior that had survived out here for years.

Hayden fought a similar battle, scrabbling around the ledge and trading blows that were never going to be effective in the enclosed space. She knocked a knife from her opponent's hand and then fell on top of it, kicked away a sidearm as he whipped it out of a holster. He punched her in the face, drawing blood.

Then Kinimaka hit at full pelt. Hayden's opponent flew helplessly, arms caught underneath him. He hit the ground on his face, smashing bone. Kinimaka landed on him, smashing more, grinding broken bones together. The man screamed. Kinimaka rose and came down with a knife, burying it through the nape of the man's neck.

Hayden rose. Alicia fought on her knees, struggling to match her opponent's strength and using his weight against him. As he missed with one heavy blow, she swung him so that his back faced the long drop. When he re-launched his body at her she jumped into the air, then kicked out, unleashing every ounce of strength in her body. The soles of her feet struck the man in the chest and sent him flying over the ledge and into space.

His scream followed him down.

Drake kept watch. There had been three climbers.

Without waiting, Hayden and Alicia began their ascent, joining him in less than a minute. Kinimaka waited. Kenzie and Dallas appeared further to the right. Dahl and Molokai were at a stalemate, unable to climb higher as the two Marauders up top hounded them.

Kinimaka abandoned his ledge and started up. Drake saw the third climber then, just creeping over the top, and sent a well-placed bullet between his eyes. This time there were no screams as the man fell.

But that left the two men at the summit. It wouldn't be long before they realized they were clear to throw grenades again. Drake said as much through the comms and then leapt at the rock wall, climbing fast. Dahl and Molokai concentrated their bullets up there, and were joined by Kenzie and Dallas.

Alicia and Hayden followed Drake, with Kinimaka moving slower to cover them.

Again, Drake climbed with abandon, trying to forget he wasn't the best climber in the group. Twelve feet from the top, and then eight. Alicia hot on his trail. Hayden to the left. *It's a race*, he thought, to calm the nerves. A team challenge. When he was four feet from the summit one of the Marauders saw him.

Crap!

He jumped, his body in mid-air for entire seconds, then reached out and grabbed an outcrop at the very top of the cliff. Luckily, both hands caught it and he hauled his body upward. But a quick glance at the Marauder told him the man was already aiming his gun.

Shots rifled his body. Blood gouted. The Marauder fell dead, killed by one of the others. Drake heaved himself over the top.

To be faced by the second man.

Holding two grenades.

"Fuck off!" Drake was close enough to kick out the man's knees, hearing cartilage pop. There was a scream, then the body struck the ground. Both grenades bounced out of his hands, springs snapping free, the pineapple-shaped bombs rolling away. Drake grabbed one and threw it away from his team and over the cliff, but he couldn't do anything about the second.

"Cover!"

It took every precious moment of time to grab hold of the fallen Marauder and pull hard, putting the man's body between Drake and the grenade.

The explosions were simultaneous. Drake felt his opponent riddled with shrapnel, heard the deadly fragments impacting against a flak jacket but also hitting the exposed face and legs. The man died hard. Drake kicked him away and rose to his knees.

Alicia rolled over the top, closely followed by Hayden. Both had their guns ready, unsure what they would find. Drake saw, across the gap, that the men on the opposite ridge were hustling away.

They would be back.

"Tell the others it's clear," he panted. "We should get away from these cliffs as fast as we can. We got lucky."

"Don't celebrate yet," Hayden said as she waved the others up. "That valley down there belongs to the Scavengers—the worst of the worst. And we're crossing it next."

CHAPTER TEN

Karin Blake chased after Mai and Luther as they raced out of the cavern. The big military blade in her hand didn't feel right—the entire situation was surreal. Luther was shrugging into a backpack, loaded with supplies. Dino was at her back, carrying a similar blade.

How the hell had it come to this?

Their captors had freed them back in the large cave, only to tell them they had a five-minute head start, after which fourteen mercenaries and four trophy hunter civilians would come tearing down the passageways, seeking their heads. They also mentioned that the cave system they traversed was part of a volcano and that the only way out was up.

Mai was running at the front. Luther called out to her: "Don't forget, they set traps ahead."

The Japanese woman didn't answer. The tunnel ran level for a while, its rock walls smooth as if formed by rushing water. Or lava?

The way was lit by the occasional torch set into the rock face above their heads. Soon, they would have to stop to take stock of the backpack's contents, but first Karin assumed Mai wanted to put as much distance between them and their pursuers as possible.

Gunshots signaled the start of the pursuit. Karin ducked her head but needn't have bothered. The passage twisted sharp right ahead and then to the left before they were running straight again.

At the next turn, Mai stopped. Luther flung the pack to the floor, crouched and unstrapped it. He muttered a quick inventory.

"Four bottles of water. Lots of snack bars. Chocolate. Big flashlight and four smaller ones, all functional. Length of rope. A few pitons." He shrugged. "That's about it."

Mai kept quiet, moving away to urge them on. As she ran down the passageway, Karin turned to stare at Dino, assessing the man. He'd taken a few knocks back at the estate where they'd been captured.

When Wu died.

Karin forced the thought and the image aside. It couldn't help her now. She heard Luther cautioning Mai against going too fast—the climb would take many hours—and felt the pace slow a little.

"You okay?" she asked her closest friend.

"Yeah, fine. Still better than you."

"Stop that shit for a minute, will you? Are you in pain?"

"I don't think it's shit." Dino panted as he ran and talked. "Just healthy competition. And, if you must know, I took a few hits to the shins and ankles when I went down. Just bruising, but it hurts like a bastard."

"Shake it off." Karin turned as the passage headed down.

"All right, Taylor."

She shook her head. Dino was nothing if he wasn't always ribbing her, trying to get a rise. They were intensely competitive and, until now, she'd believed that a good thing. She just hoped it wouldn't force the crazy Italian-American to do something stupid.

Her own feelings were a mess. From losing Ben and her parents to the old Blood King just a few years ago, to finding Komodo and falling for him. The gentle giant's death in Hong Kong at the hands of the Yakuza had destroyed her spirit and her faith in the human race for a long time. She'd used Drake to get her a place in a regime where she could forget everything, where she could lose herself. Where pain and bloodshed and desperate longing all melded into one.

In the end, it turned out to be the best decision of her life. Though not without its own pitfalls. Wracked with guilt and nursing a hatred for Drake and the SPEAR team, she had allowed the new regime to change her, hone her into a revenge-fuelled machine. She'd grown close to Dino and Wu. Had she deliberately used them? Karin didn't like to think about that ever since they were tagged as deserters and, now, Wu was dead.

Where next?

Survive.

It was all she could do. Survive everything before her. She had enrolled in the new Blood King's army—hating every moment of it—just to get close to Kovalenko and learn his plans for the future. In the end, he'd second-guessed her, bringing the schedule forward without telling her. To her mind, that was what got Wu, Smyth and Lauren killed. Her failure.

Karin forged on now, following Luther. The big man was a welcome presence, exuding experience and security.

Mai slowed as a large chamber appeared ahead. It was well lit and opened out to both sides, almost circular with a high ceiling. A wide stream ran across the middle. Luther pointed ahead, and Mai nodded. They all saw the exit, a ragged arch on the opposite side, its entrance black with shadow. Karin still couldn't hear any signs of pursuit but assumed their hunters were coming.

In single-file they jumped the stream, landing safely on the other side. Dino dropped his knife but collected it without incident. As he bent down, he winced.

Mai walked over to his side. "Dig in," she said. "Learn to like it. There's no stopping and no hanging around. If they catch us, we're dead."

"You can rest when you're dead," Luther growled.

Mai moved out, heading straight for the dark exit arch. Beyond, it was pitch-black. No more wall torches. The Japanese woman waited for Luther to pass her the large flashlight and then started walking. Karin flicked on a smaller one, shining it at the floor to see her way ahead. The sudden darkness was not a welcome addition.

Another chamber followed, this one partly lit. The floor was littered with rubbish—old cans and wrappers, even a box of cards. It was clear some mercs used this place as a getaway, but it was also clear the Devil and the Blood King were aware of its existence.

More tunnels stretched ahead, alternating between declines and inclines, but Karin judged the general way was up. When a fiery glow lit up the tunnel walls ahead, Mai was forced to slow.

"Don't like the look of that," Luther whispered.

"No choice," Mai responded.

"I know. I just don't like the look of it."

They rounded a corner to see a drop off to the right, just a narrow wedge of empty space. That in itself put Karin on her guard—were there more holes ahead, and could they be in the middle of the path? But this was different—the empty space was alight. Roiling red and orange light flashed up from below.

When Karin inched closer she looked down about forty feet. Lava flowed very slowly down there, a thick mass of fire that rolled and inched its way along. The heat as she leaned out was intense, catching in her throat.

Karin coughed and pulled away. Quickly, they left the lava tube behind and moved on, seeking fresher air. Several more minutes passed without any sounds of pursuit. As Mai turned a sharp, dark corner she came to an abrupt stop, holding up a hand. Luther halted but Karin walked into his back, and Dino into hers.

"Stop," Mai hissed.

"Trap?" Luther asked, not mentioning the collisions.

"Claymore," she said. "Very rudimentary. I guess they thought it's in the darkest part of the passage, around a corner."

"Or the traps aren't meant to kill us," Luther said. "Just slow us down."

"Yeah," Dino agreed. "They're saving us for the great white trophy hunters."

"Which is their mistake." Luther reached down to disarm the mine, but Mai grabbed his hand.

"No. Leave it for them."

He smiled back. "I was going to disarm it and move it," he said, "nearer to the lava cavern."

Karin nodded, seeing the cunning in that thought. Their enemies might think the device had been removed and taken for later use, or disarmed and hidden, but moved closer . . . ?

Not quite as likely.

Mai waited a few seconds for Luther to make the explosive safe and head back the way they came. Then she hurried on, knowing he would catch up. Karin stayed close and heard Dino panting along behind. Their world was composed of an archway of rock, darkness in every direction, with just a few pools of light to guide their way. So far, there had been no junctions providing other tunnels to follow.

Soon, Luther re-joined them, and it was with a whispered warning. "Heard them back there. They're coming fast."

"Not taking care?" Mai asked, interested.

"It didn't sound like it."

The Japanese woman nodded, storing away the information. It felt odd, but here, now, Karin deferred every decision to Mai. She was a legend, a hero. She'd seen and done everything imaginable, encountered all scenarios.

Karin might be military trained, but she wasn't nearly in the same league as Mai. And more importantly, Karin trusted her with her life.

And Dino's.

Moving faster, they forged on.

CHAPTER ELEVEN

The Devil sat before his console array, familiarizing himself with events transpiring in Washington DC, and in the life of the Dahls, before contacting his men. Several nuggets of information had been uncovered since their last conversation. There was a parade being organized for the day of the operation. It was close enough to the girls' school to be useful and, more importantly, Johanna—the mother—had been checking it out on the Internet. It appeared she wanted to go.

In addition to that, the parade bordered on a darker part of town, where civil unrest was easy to fuel.

The Devil ran the various factors through his mind. He'd done something like this before but that was in Cairo, a wholly different and a far easier prospect. Still, the fundamentals were the same. Find a parade, fuel hatred, start a riot—people die.

Or they get trampled or . . . whatever. It didn't matter to the Devil. He nodded with satisfaction and then studied the monitors dedicated to watching the main house. Nothing had changed.

The Devil contacted his two men on the ground for their reports. Afterward he began to speak: "You have to escalate a riot cautiously before the parade. Don't rush it. But make it critical. Do you know how to do that?"

Yes, they did. It usually involved murder.

"Start immediately. I want everything moving right away. Don't miss this deadline. It's everything we've waited for."

A few minutes later he signed off and turned his attention to events happening around the island. Luka Kovalenko was leaving. Not a bad thing. There was a tension between them, something not alleviated by the Devil's own willingness to hide the Blood King for several days. He thought Kovalenko might fear him. Feared what he could do. Not a bad position to be in, truth be told, but not the best either.

He also knew what Luka could do. The men were better enemies than friends, but the Devil hoped they could keep a respectful distance for now.

In the past he'd taken out worse than the old Blood King. He'd even turned down a job to neutralize the man himself, considering it too dangerous, too messy. The Devil had to think about his own reputation, and general obscurity, as much as his clients'. Still, he had to admit the challenge it presented had excited him.

Now, he watched Kovalenko's fast speedboat transport him from the island to the large yacht that waited offshore. Good riddance to the man and his convoluted plans. It would be a while before the Devil heard from him again—his next operation was months away from fruition.

The jetty and the dock areas were busy. Two dozen mercs were loading supplies and packing crates full of merchandise to sell around Europe. *Contraband*, the Devil thought and laughed. His men made conversation and moved slowly. The Devil wished he had a remote machine gun he could use to put some fire into them. Time was money, and the latter was in short supply of late.

Still, everything was about to get better.

His base of operations was changing. The escape plan was foolproof. One of the reasons he'd allowed Kovalenko to use his island to prepare the mini nukes was knowing he could rid himself of the massive problem that the island had become in just one magnificent blow. He would destroy it and every terrible creature that crawled upon its surface.

Kovalenko just left, which leaves me twenty-four hours.

Preparations were well underway. His deliberations were interrupted by a slave, knocking at the door and bowing for attention.

"What is it?"

"I have been asked to find out which of the slaves and captives you wish to take, sir."

The Devil hesitated. It was a good question. The prisoners were so far beneath his thinking he hadn't even considered them. "Women and children will fetch the best prices," he said. "Nothing old though. Some of the younger men too. The rest—" he paused, then grinned "—set them free right before we leave. That will build their hopes up before the nuke goes off."

"Yes, sir." The middle-aged slave backed away, probably knowing that it would be forced to stay behind.

The Devil laughed again. There was something invigorating about having absolute power. One of his scouts had reported that he'd found an abandoned town somewhere in the US, a remote ghost town. He'd thought about calling it Devil's Junction and moving there. Maybe that time would come.

The Devil watched Kovalenko's big yacht turn and make ready to sail. It was then, whilst watching and debating the new Blood King's merits and failings, that a fresh thought occurred to him.

That fucker would double cross me in a heartbeat.

No, that wasn't quite right. Luka would double cross him only if he thought he'd die. And the niggle was that Luka had sent the signal to arm the nuke before departing. The

Devil frowned, not quite trusting his own thoughts. He was the Devil. Nobody in their right mind would cross him.

But Luka Kovalenko was a man apart.

Cursing softly, surprised at himself for such depth of paranoia, he left the office and headed downstairs. His keep, the central building of the castle, consisted of a high, winding staircase and two rooms. At the top, his surveillance room. His castle within a castle. The keep was surrounded by four other buildings which provided bedrooms, meeting rooms and eating places. The walls surrounded all that; thick crenelated bastions that kept the islanders at bay.

He walked into the morning light, the air too cool for his tastes. He had become accustomed to the afternoon heat. He walked past the compound to the furthest building. Inside was a secret bunker. Well, maybe not so secret. By necessity, several of his men knew its location. And so did Kovalenko. The Blood King and three of his men had carried the small nuke down there.

The Devil tried hard to shrug off a mixed feeling of suspicion and apprehension as he descended a set of black-iron steps into a dusty, empty cellar and walked over to a hidden keypad.

But the feeling wouldn't go away.

CHAPTER TWELVE

Three hours had passed since they made landfall.

Drake crouched low as Molokai, ahead, raised a fist. They were creeping along a deep ditch. A brown sludgy stream ran down the center. The grassy verges were steep, sometimes muddy, but made great screens. Molokai scrambled back.

"I think we should stop here for refreshment," he said. "The land is well traveled ahead, and we might not get chance for a while."

His meaning was clear. Having left the cliffs behind, the team had entered the valley area that belonged to the Scavengers—the worst clan on the island. So far, they hadn't found any signs of life—but that could soon change.

Drake leaned back on the grass verge, his legs propped up on the other side. Alicia joined him, rooting through his pack to grab water and food. Drake waited, reflecting on the cliff battle. They had all come through without too many bruises, but then the cover had been good. His team had survived, but every time they confronted an enemy he worried. As a soldier, he knew that was wrong. He didn't have the time nor the luxury to worry. And, if you let it eat away at you, it could become a far worse enemy than any twenty-stone merc with an Uzi.

He ate now and sipped water. They consulted the map. They were crossing at the north end of the valley primarily because it was a more direct route to the high mountain where Mai should be. *We hope.* Everything on this island was an unknown quantity. But they were here and maybe, with luck, they'd find the Devil and Kovalenko here too.

Molokai pinpointed their position on the map. Dahl took a quick recce. The team made sure their weapons were fully loaded. They harbored no illusions as to how hard it would be to cross Scavenger territory.

Drake waited impatiently for the others to make ready.

"Don't worry," Alicia said. "We'll get there in time. Have faith."

He had great faith in the team. "It's all the other bastards that worry me. I mean, how the hell did we get thrown onto an island inhabited by wild killer-mercs?"

"Cheer up." Dahl grinned. "At least it's not dinosaurs."

Drake gave him a hard stare. Molokai rose at the head of the pack, which everyone took as a sign to leave.

"Slow ahead," he said through the comms. "No sound now."

They used the ditch to progress further before creeping up to the top and surveying the area. The sun had risen over the horizon and was bathing the landscape with light, which was both good and bad for the SPEAR team. Because of the unique shape of the valley, its folding contours, they were able to crawl to the top of a rolling hill and look down toward the center.

The Scavengers weren't exactly hiding.

Their camp lay at the base of a dip near the center of the lush green hills. Sentry posts were visible on nearby slopes, but they didn't appear to spread far and wide. Harrison had mentioned that the other clans gave the Scavengers a wide berth, which probably accounted for the more localized security. Using field glasses, the team scanned the camp and looked for ways they might bypass it.

But it was the camp itself that held their attention for far longer than it should have.

The Scavengers lived in makeshift lean-tos or in badly

dug holes in the ground. They walked around or slept in various states of dress. They were all unwashed and, from what Drake saw, bore untreated wounds and cuts over their bodies.

Molokai spotted a better vantage point to the left and signaled. Taking extreme caution, the team slid their way into position.

"Holy shit," Hayden whispered.

Drake could hardly believe his eyes. Wild dogs slunk through the camp, sometimes petted by the dirty-faced men. Fires burned outside several lean-tos, and there was a large blaze at the center of the camp. Smoke billowed into the air, marking their position. Drake saw that, beyond the camp, lay the wide blue snake of a rushing river, and assumed fresh water was plentiful for these people. Switching back to the camp he forced himself to take in the worst of what was down there.

Wooden crosses had been dug into the ground. Men were strapped to them. Their heads hung low and they flinched as if in the throes of a nightmare. Drake could easily believe it. Their bare chests and legs had been flayed but they bled only sparingly, as if the wounds had been seared by fire.

Other men were in chains, thrown together at the edge of the camp. The iron manacles weighed them down, placed over wrists, ankles and necks, forcing them together into a twisted heap that could barely move. Scavengers walked past and laughed at their predicament, throwing stones, spitting or taking out a well-sharpened blade and stabbing at the desperate pile. As Drake watched he heard a man shout a command. One of the dogs ran at the bunch of chained men and leapt on them, jaws gnashing. When it finished, several more were bleeding.

Alicia lowered her field glasses. "Looks like hell down there."

"They're men who've lost touch with civilization," Dahl said. "And revel in savagery."

"Look to the top right," Kenzie murmured.

Drake twisted his body and refocused. The sight sent cold water through his body. Several sharpened stakes were set at the crest of a hill. Each stake was topped with a severed head in varying states of decomposition.

"Warnings," Dahl said.

"Let's heed them," Hayden said. "What's the best way through?"

Molokai looked over. "Around," he said. "The best way is around."

"Can we afford the time?"

Molokai and Dahl both indicated the rushing waters.

"If we can get to the river further north," the Swede said. "We could go faster."

"You think they have boats? Rafts maybe?"

Dahl started crawling to the left. "Why wouldn't they?"

Because they're fucking batshit crazy, Drake wanted to say but held his tongue.

The next thirty minutes passed in a tense, edgy silence. The team hugged the slopes, keeping eight feet of incline between them and any sight of the camp below. Kenzie was wary of several thick trees they passed, worried about Scavenger lookouts. The team took a few minutes to scan all of them but saw no sign of any watchers. Drake tried to compartmentalize everything he'd seen below and concentrate on the way forward, but it was almost impossible. Of course, those prisoners would be members of similar clans, prone to the same tendencies, but they were still human.

Or had been before they were tortured.

Forty minutes after they started to circumvent the Scavenger camp, they heard raised voices. Drake cursed silently and raised his gun. Dahl shimmied fast to the top of the slope.

"It's not for us," he said. "It's . . . well, shit, come and look."

Drake was close on his heels. He glanced over the top. Below, he counted eighteen men—almost the entire Scavenger clan. They had formed a circle and were shouting, grunting, urging each other on.

Axes were flung to the center of the circle. Bare-chested men leapt at them, raising and brandishing them. They yelled something unintelligible. They came forward, smashing their axe-heads together with a deep clang. They shuffled and bowed as their clan mates grunted. Four stood in the center of the circle, axes whirling.

Drake wondered how men could become so debased. The axes swung closer and closer to the men on the crosses. Those men had now come awake, eyes filled with terror as they tried to pull away.

"Are we helping them?" Dallas asked.

Alicia regarded him. "Shit, you sound like the Sprite. Don't forget everyone's an animal down there."

"Yeah, but—"

"Ordinarily I'd say yes," Hayden said, aware that Kinimaka would feel the same way as Dallas. "But Mai and the others, the Devil and Kovalenko, have to take priority now. We can come back to this later."

They lingered a little longer, wincing as the blades struck and blood ran. It was only when four more men lit torches and brought those flaming beacons into the circle, close to the bleeding men, that Molokai slithered back down the slope and decided to lead the way.

Around.

Drake and Dahl followed him. The sounds from the camp intensified: screaming punctuated by laughter and manic yelling. The noise the Scavengers made was savage, straight from a maniac's nightmare.

Ahead, the dip they were following rose to the top of another slope. There were no more dips.

"River shouldn't be far away," Molokai said.

Drake checked his watch. "Four hours gone. I hope we're in bloody time."

CHAPTER THIRTEEN

Mai hurried through the tunnels as fast as she dared. Conscious of their pursuers, the hazards of the passages and potential booby traps, her attention was focused on their upward course. She left Luther to worry about slowing their followers down and watching out for Karin and Dino.

She became aware of a change ahead as air flowed past more quickly, musty but relatively fresh. It gave her the same sense that entering a large cavern did, and she wasn't disappointed. Their tunnel widened, the roof disappearing above. She ran into a vast cave, dissected by a large gap. Mai edged closer and grimaced, gauging it to be at least twelve feet wide.

"I'm not jumping that," Luther said. "I could . . . but I'm not."

"Yeah, me too." Mai scanned the area. The cavern was lit by torches, revealing that the hunters wanted to see what happened in this cave. Presumably though, they didn't want the chase to end in the first few hours. The hunt was part of their sport and had no doubt been planned down to the last detail.

"Ideas?" Mai asked.

A gust of wind swept the cave as she spoke, making the torch flames gutter. Darkness and then light crossed her features.

"Can we hold them off a while?" Dino asked.

"With these?" Luther brandished his knife.

"We need some of their guns."

Mai agreed with the young man's thought processes but couldn't let him act on impulse. "That'll come," she said. "For now, we have to maintain our lead."

"I can jump that," Dino speculated. Karin laid a hand on his arm.

Mai pointed at the ceiling where it lowered as it crossed the center of the gap. "There's that, but . . ."

Luther whistled. "It's risky."

Mai knelt and opened the backpack. "More like suicide," she said.

Karin dropped to her side. "You can't be serious?"

"I really think she is." Dino was standing at the edge of the precipice, eyeing the ceiling. "It might even work."

Mai heaved out the length of rope and let it unravel onto the floor. "Now," she said. "Who can throw a lasso?"

She looked at Luther, who spread his arms. "Hey, just because I'm American doesn't mean I'm a fucking cowboy."

Mai tied one end of the rope into a lasso and began to coil the rest around one arm. Dino stepped up. "I've done this before."

Mai counted the minutes passing. "One chance," she said. "Do it."

Dino took the rope, aimed and threw it toward the ceiling where a rock feature formed the shape of a crude hook. The rope fell short, its end slithering into the black crevice.

Mai held out a hand. "I'll do it."

"No, no, I can do it." Dino was busy reeling in the abrasive twine and planting his feet for a second go.

"We don't have time for this," Luther grated.

Before they could stop him, Dino had coiled the rope, steadied himself and let the lasso go once again. This time the looped end fell over the hook of rock. Dino gave a cheer as he tightened it.

"Doubt you could've done that, Blake."

Karin was busy retying the backpack. "Let's see you jump it now, Dino."

Mai pushed them firmly aside. "I'll go first, Luther last. You two kids can argue about who comes next."

Without waiting, and ignoring Dino's wince of anxiety, she pulled on the rope and swung across the twelve-foot wide gap. First, she took a run up, then grabbed the rope and jumped, using momentum to swing across to the other side Once there, she landed on two feet, kept hold of the rope, then turned and swung it back across.

"Hurry!"

Luther was at the entrance to the cavern. "I don't hear anything."

Mai estimated they'd lost three minutes. Their hunters couldn't be too far behind, even assuming they'd lost time disarming the Claymore. Karin grabbed the returning rope, gave Dino an impish look, and followed Mai's example. She landed safely. Mai grabbed the rope and gave it back to her.

"Take charge of this. I'm scouting ahead."

Karin threw the rope back to Dino as Mai left. It was Luther's voice that stopped her. Low pitched, so only they could hear, it was the only noise in the cave.

"I hear them."

Mai paused, but what could she do? Throw rocks at them? Her skills were honed to the highest level but even she couldn't make that work. It was then she noticed Dino and the run up he took.

"Wait, that's not . . . !"

But Dino was already sprinting, conscious that they were hard-pressed. He didn't seem to be aware that his run-up wasn't long enough. Karin saw it and ran to the edge of the gap. Mai backed her up. Dino was already in flight, hanging on tight, face set as hard as the granite around them.

When he let go, his feet fell short of the far surface. He let out a grunt, trying to fling his body at the edge. He didn't make it. Karin leapt forward as Dino started to plummet down the shaft.

"Nooo!"

Mai felt her heart sink; her blood freeze. They'd already lost too many good people and now another. She saw Karin toppling over the edge, reaching out too far for Dino and unbalancing. Mai jumped onto the back of Karin's legs.

And Luther, cringing at the whole scene, knew there was a single, fleeting chance to gain the other side and escape certain death. As the empty rope swung back toward the center of the cave, the big American ran and threw himself at it, jumping out over the pitch-black crevice. His fingers and hands reached. In mid-air, he caught the rope, the momentum of his jump sending it back toward Mai. As it flew over the edge he let go, landing on his back and jarring his spine, skidding to a halt.

He spun, stopped the end of the rope swinging back, and unhooked it from the ceiling.

Mai held Karin down, wondering why she couldn't just pull her own weight back up. Then it occurred to her.

She was hanging on to Dino!

Mai shouted at Luther and together the two hauled Karin up and over the ledge. Dino came after. The Italian's head was bleeding and his eyes wary due to the dent in his pride but he was otherwise unhurt.

Karin breathed deeply. "You owe me one, mate."

Dino rolled and groaned. "Get me outta this cave and I'll happily give you one."

Luther pulled both youngsters to their feet. "Keep it clean for now," he said. "All that can come later."

Mai saw movement on the other side of the cave and ushered everyone back, toward the exit. Before their enemy appeared, they were gone, leaving no sign that they had been there or almost failed to cross.

It was a good win, she thought.

But it had been too damn close.

CHAPTER FOURTEEN

Mai knew this was the time to push hard, to take risks that would later prove valuable. It was likely that Valance and his mercs had brought along a device to make their own gap crossing far easier and quicker, but it would still slow them down. She took the flashlight and a torch and ran, illuminating the way ahead as best she could. Luther was at her shoulder, checking to left and right for cross passages. The tunnel walls curved around them, ragged rock that, if you let it, might drive you insane with claustrophobia. She had no real idea how far down they were—but it had to be a fair way.

Just the thought of all that mountain mass crushing down on her brought shivers.

She shrugged it off, not given to panic. She'd encountered far worse in her missions; to be totally honest she'd encountered worse during the odd night out with Alicia Myles. There were incalculable terrors abroad in the world today, chasing down the innocent purely because they were the weaker prey.

The air smelled dank down here. She was reminded that they were inside a volcano whenever a sulfur stench rose. Once, she heard an ominous rumble. Through it all, Luther was at her back.

"We can't keep this up for hours," Karin said.

"I know. But if we can create a good lead and find a defendable cave, then we can rest for a bit."

Luther grunted his agreement, liking her plan. The

trouble was, thirty minutes later they were still running, following a right-hard curve. It was Luther that saw something and Mai that ended up face down on the floor.

Luther tackled her about the waist, bringing his full weight to bear. Mai landed head first, striking her forehead on the rock floor, crying out in shock and pain.

"Jesus," Dino said from behind. "This really isn't the time."

Mai raised her head, anger rushing through her, but came face to face with a black tripwire. Pulled taut, it stretched across the passage less than an inch in front of her nose.

"Don't worry," Luther growled. "I can smell those bastards like bacon at a veggie market."

Mai let out a breath. "Do they make your mouth water too?"

Luther pulled her up, smiling. "Every time."

Karin was studying the contraption. "The wire leads up the wall . . . there."

Carefully, they stepped over the booby trap and gazed at the ceiling where a simple counterbalance mechanism met a wide plank of wood.

"Trip the wire and the plank comes down," Luther stared. "And those spikes give you free air conditioning. Easy."

"I wish we could use it for our friends back there," Mai said.

Luther pursed his lips. "Maybe we can rig it differently."

Three minutes later, the big American had moved the wire from ankle height to chest height. It was rudimentary but still stood a fair chance of working since their pursuers should be staring at the floor.

Luther wiped sweat from his face. "Quick prayer to the

god of booby traps, folks. Here's to big fortune with boobies."

"You religious?" Karin asked.

"Only when I need to be, Blake."

Dino was already bowing his head, a smile playing at the corner of his mouth. Mai broke it up and urged them on. They passed another lava tube, this one glowing so hot the reflection hurt their eyes. They paused to drink water and eat an energy bar. Mai leaned with her back to the side of the tunnel, Luther beside her. As she ate, a faint scream echoed along the tunnel. Luther slammed the rock with satisfaction.

"It worked."

"Nice." Mai nodded. "But that puts them only ten minutes behind us. Let's go."

"How long have we been running?" Karin asked as they moved off.

"Not long. A couple of hours."

"You know we can't keep this up forever. We're gonna have to make a stand."

"Yeah, Karin," Mai muttered. "I know that very well."

Karin fought off the aches and pains and pushed on. It was true Mai had extended the gap since they started running, but what if there was no defensible cave? They would eventually become exhausted. Every twenty steps one of them knocked a knee or barked a shin or slammed a shoulder into some rocky outcropping. There were tiny pits in the floor—ankle breakers. Stepping into one of those would shine an entirely different light on the chase.

And factor in the detail that Valance and his mercenaries gave them a head start, knowing how good Mai and Luther were. It didn't bode well. She used her torch to check for pitfalls, but it was inadequate. Her best bet was to follow Luther closely, use him as a shield against whatever dangers lay ahead.

Dino was loping along at the rear, panting but not complaining. Several times she'd caught his eye and received that cheeky little grin. Down here, it irritated her. Didn't he realize the danger they were in? Was he really that young and stupid?

Then why was she attracted to him?

It wasn't chemistry. They were opposites, she thought. Rivals even. Dino competed with her every step of the way. They clashed. Fought like siblings. The only thing she could put her finger on was their time together. It had fuelled a kind of twisted allure. She couldn't get it out of her head.

Dino? Never!

He was immature, too young for her. *Hey, you have needs. Just use him for a while.* But that would just change their dynamic and, much as she complained, she thought they made a good team.

Back on the container, as they sailed ever nearer Devil's Island, two men had started to mess with her. They'd made sure Luther and Mai were properly secured over the other side of the container and then approached, leering, their eyes revealing their intentions. Karin had never seen them before that day, and it wasn't meal time, so she'd assumed they'd sneaked in, intent on hateful deeds.

The first, a ginger-bearded giant with tiny eyes, grabbed her ankles and pulled her toward them. Karin's chains tightened around her wrists and neck, forcing her arms over her head and her face upward. She struggled, tried to scream, but the manacle around her neck prevented all sound. It was all she could do to breathe. Luther and Mai were struggling with their bonds on the opposite side of the container.

The second man, a whip-thin individual with a creepy smile, just stared at them. Ginger Beard hissed in his direction.

"Grab her leg, Gipper. She's a fighter."

Both men struggled. Even as she choked Karin fought them, striking a chin or a cheekbone with her shins and boots. Mai and Luther shouted death threats and fought their bonds, but it was Dino that saved her. The Italian started with an attack, as she would expect. His flying feet caught both men off guard, drawing blood. They jumped on him and punched his stomach hard again and again, draining all the air from him until he could do nothing but lay there gasping.

Then they returned to her.

"Same thing?" Gipper asked in an oily voice.

"Works for me."

They fell upon her, one to each side, but Dino recovered faster than they anticipated. Instead of attacking, he must have fought every instinct and shouted for help. Screaming. Banging on the container's sides and bellowing for the guards. He smashed his head against the steel before thinking to use the chains.

Within minutes their normal captors arrived, annoyed, to see what the hell was going on. Ginger Beard and Gipper were kicked across the floor, never to be seen again.

Karin wouldn't forget the sight of Dino, mad with rage at the treatment she was getting, selflessly fighting for her, ready to receive bone-breaking retaliation or worse, just to save her.

Now, he tapped her on the shoulder. "Love those two," he said, nodding at Mai and Luther. "Legends."

She gritted her teeth, annoyed but knowing what he meant. "Just stay quiet," she said. "And try to keep up."

"With you? Not a problem."

"When we get out of here," she said. "I'm gonna challenge you to a combat and endurance test. We'll see who comes first."

Dino went wide-eyed. "Is that your way of asking me to . . . you know . . ."

Karin ground her teeth together in anger, but couldn't stop the grin from forming. "Dino, you're a bloody idiot."

"I know."

The tunnel sloped upward for a while before angling to the left, which became a long loop. The sounds of pursuit fell away. Someone had died back there, she was sure of it, and it had slowed their pursuers down.

Score one to the good guys. But that still left thirteen armed mercs and four gun-toting civilians at their backs, not to mention a ticking time bomb. It didn't look good.

Karin continued to trust Mai and follow in her footsteps.

CHAPTER FIFTEEN

Drake forced down lurid visions of what the Scavengers were doing to their prisoners and even to themselves. The verdant valley slopes ran gently toward the wide, fast-flowing river. Dahl was ahead, staying low, scanning their surrounds. Everyone else was prone, leaving nothing to chance.

The Swede turned to wave at them.

"Use the comms," Drake whispered. "It's easier."

Dahl gave him the finger. "But this is quicker."

They made their way to the edge of the river, conscious that the slopes led back to the Scavenger site and overlooked their position. Wild, rushing water crashed past to the left, smoothing away the banks and taking debris with it. Branches, bits of rotten wood, and even a tree trunk flowed along its undulating middle.

"According to the map, that river leads away from Scavenger territory and past the base of the mountain," Dallas said. "If we follow it . . ."

Molokai and Kenzie were studying something in the distance. "You said we were in a hurry," the Israeli said. "There's your answer."

Drake squinted. Four black shapes, alien to the landscape, were just visible near the banks of the river. When he realized what they were he nodded. "Four dinghies," he said. "Stacked high."

Hayden was already walking toward them. The rest followed, studying every inch of landscape. They made it without incident. As they approached, Drake saw they were military issue Zodiacs, the best the Army used. Alicia and Kinimaka stepped forward, untying ropes and heaving the boats to the ground.

"That's enough," Hayden said when two had been untied. "Let's get them onto the river."

Drake watched their backs, using the rifle's sights to check faraway hills and his eyes to check the nearer ones. A hot mid-morning breeze sent beads of sweat popping along his forehead. The soil here was loamy, soft underfoot. The rushing waters of the river overwhelmed everything, dulling the senses. Dahl was at his side, checking the other bank, watching the trees that lined its route over there.

"We have a problem," Drake said.

"Yep, looks like there was a guard watching the Zodiacs." Dahl looked over. "Or they were left as a deliberate trap."

Kinimaka jumped into the river, trying to hold fast as the water tore at his legs. Molokai waded in alongside him. Together, they dragged two boats into the river as Alicia and Kenzie pushed. When they gained some momentum, the women jumped in.

"Hurry!"

Drake saw the Scavengers coming. Bare chested and screaming, they surged down one slope and then over the top of the next hill. All carried automatic weapons as well as axes. Two carried human heads that dripped blood. Together, he and Dahl opened fire. Their bullets passed among the running men without any acknowledgement.

Kenzie and Dallas jumped into a boat with Alicia. Hayden, Kinimaka and Molokai took the second. Dahl turned and ran to Hayden's, whilst Drake leapt to the right of Alicia's gun.

"Jump!" The dinghy was drifting, starting to gain momentum.

Drake grabbed hold of the webbing that covered the

boat's exterior and hauled his body up. Cold water made him gasp. Dallas helped pull him inside. Alicia's shots were loud in his right ear.

"You tag any yet?"

"Nah. Too much movement."

It wasn't just the chaotic pace of their enemy, it was now also the bobbing boat that affected her aim. As it drifted more to the center of the river the boat picked up speed. Drake used a paddle to push off an overhanging tree. The Scavengers were nearing the shore but threw themselves to the ground as the whole SPEAR team opened fire.

Bullets slammed into the earth and the grassy banks, even into the mud at the sides of the river. Men rolled for cover, some firing back. The men carrying the severed heads hung on to them despite the danger.

Drake turned his attention ahead. The river had whipped them into a headlong rush. The center was fast, an unstoppable current. To his right, Alicia shouted that the Scavengers were untying the other boats.

"Crap," Hayden said. "We can do without that."

"You reckon?" Alicia tried to sight in on an enemy, but the momentum of the boat made her body shift to the right. She rolled right into Kenzie.

"Are you kidding, Myles? Here? Now?"

"You really think you're my type, bitch?"

Dahl, from the other boat, shouted: "What? Crazy, deranged, disorganized and daft as a brush? Yeah, that's you."

"Hey!" Drake shouted. "I'm not deranged."

Alicia rolled away from Kenzie. "Yeah, Dahl, talk about hitting several people with one shot."

Dahl bowed. "I know, but I really am that good."

Kenzie glared over at the Swede. Drake stared at the

Scavengers. Already, they'd dragged their boats into the water and were climbing in. He counted six men per boat. It would slow them down, but not enough.

"Dallas," he said. "Watch where we're going. Everyone else, fancy some target practice?"

They lay across the back of the boat, taking aim. To the right and twenty feet behind, the second boat skimmed the surging waters. White froth flew between them. Spray dampened them. Drake heard Dallas start the boat and felt the steering take hold. Hayden did the same.

"Y'know something," Drake heard Dallas say to Kenzie. "When I queued up to join your mercenary team I knew your reputation. I knew there'd be wild times. But never in my craziest dreams could I have imagined everything that's happened."

"Hey," Kenzie leaned over. "What can I say? I give good ... um, value."

Alicia cackled. Drake fired a quick burst, worrying now what might happen if Alicia and Kenzie ever became friends. His attention was thankfully diverted when the Scavengers returned fire.

Bullets flew between the boats. Most flew past, but Drake heard several smash into the Zodiac's hull. The river started to turn, a long sweeping bend, which upset everyone's aim once more. Drake guessed they were only a hundred feet ahead of their pursuers, which meant one mistake would bring them alongside.

On a brighter note, they were now rushing across the island at great speed.

The Zodiacs navigated the wide, rushing flow, engines roaring, taking the broad bend at a pace that raised the right bottom lips of their boats. Men lay on their stomachs inside, raising their heads occasionally to take potshots or use their weapons on full auto, raking the splashing waters, the tree-lined banks and the rolling hills beyond. Drake tried targeting an enemy, but it was no use. The chase was too frantic.

Dallas yelled, "That's not good, hang on!"

Drake cringed, unable to see and not knowing what to expect. The nose of the Zodiac dipped and then the entire craft shot down. Foaming water appeared at both sides. They skidded left and right, and he understood.

They had hit a rough section of river rapids. Fountains of spray splashed over them, soaking his hair and face. He wiped his eyes dry pointlessly as the boat skimmed over several rocks to the right and fell again, soaking the entire boat as it plummeted down into crashing waves. Dahl's boat came after, turning dangerously, but glanced off their bows. Dallas lurched to the side but held on as everyone slammed into each other. Dallas opened the throttle.

The boat surged ahead, away from the set of rapids and a surging whirlpool of water, but straight into another. Drake saw the Scavengers coming down the rapids now, much more calmly, still firing their weapons.

Of course, they'd know about the rapids and used them to close the gap.

There was no time to think. They hit the second set of rapids and this one was much more severe. The Zodiac tipped to the right. Dallas would have fallen out, dashed against the underwater rocks if Kenzie hadn't snagged his jacket with her arm and pulled him back. Even then, she cried out with the pain of a pulled muscle. Dallas fell over her. The boat slammed down onto its base. It was pulled sideways until its stern faced forward and then, suddenly, fell through thin air.

Alicia cried out in shock. Drake grabbed some webbing

and hung on, yelling, reminded of years of rollercoaster rides. The free-fall seemed to last forever, but it was only seconds. They hit water hard, spinning again. Dallas scrambled up to the front. Drake received knocks to the head and the ribs, but was able to raise his head just in time to see Dahl's boat fall down the short drop.

Part of him wanted to see the Swede hanging on for his life, face tight with fear, screaming his throat raw. What he got was Dahl calmly firing at their pursuers and ignoring the drop.

Drake shook his head. "Show off thinks he's in a bloody movie."

Dahl's boat hit the bottom of the steep drop. Both Scavengers' boats slid over just seconds later. Drake aimed, seeing an opportunity. As both boats dropped, its occupants slid into clearer view. Alicia fired at his side. Together they shot two Scavengers and saw them reel back in pain and shock. Blood splashed the inside of their Zodiac. By the time they hit the bottom they were flopping, falling about. Within seconds their comrades had unceremoniously dumped their bodies over the side.

More shots were exchanged. It took Dallas a little while but soon he coaxed the Zodiac away from the rocks and was directing her back out into the middle of the river. They gained speed.

Dahl's craft followed, still commanded by Hayden with Molokai, Dahl and Kinimaka taking shots at the enemy. Drake watched, anxious until they attained some momentum again. The Scavengers drifted close to them but weren't firing.

Instead, they were climbing onto the rim of their boat, ready to pounce. They had axes and knives in their hands.

Drake opened fire, wounding one man, but it wasn't

enough. Hayden opened the throttle fully, sending her Zodiac lurching forward. Dahl was thrown out into the water and onto the nearest bank, slamming his head against the ground. The Scavengers leapt into Hayden's boat. Molokai and Kinimaka rose to meet them.

"Stop!" Drake cried. "Turn around."

But Dallas struggled. He could cut the engine, possibly turn the boat, but he couldn't fight the flow of the surging river. The current grabbed them. Drake saw the second Scavenger boat slam into Hayden's craft, its occupants already jumping across to join the fight. He made ready to dive overboard.

"Don't." Kenzie laid a hand on his arm. "You'll be swept downstream."

It was true, but what the hell else could he do? There were ten Scavengers against Hayden, Kinimaka and Molokai. He saw men hurled into the air, into the river and against submerged rocks. He saw more tossed overboard.

But it wasn't enough.

The Scavengers had the numbers. They had guns too, which they trained on Hayden and then on the others. It didn't work at first.

Molokai launched his bulk at the enemy, sending five overboard, but the others battered him with their guns and knife-hilts, keeping him down. Those in the water raised weapons and fired. Hayden ducked. Kinimaka took a shot to the vest, which sent him to his knees. The enemy piled on.

Hayden moved to help but fell as a man rolled into her. More Scavengers climbed into their boat, rocking it dangerously. Dahl, upstream a little, still hadn't moved. Dallas fought the river's momentum, finally managing to point their craft at the bank. It still bounced downstream with the river but edged sideways.

Drake kept up constant fire, unable to hit bodies at this distance. He saw Kinimaka rising up, bloodied, fighting hard, but then three men jumped onto his back. Molokai had a similar problem, with four men hanging onto him.

Behind, easily visible because of the plumb-straight river, they saw Hayden, Kinimaka and Molokai dragged at gunpoint across the rapids and into the trees that covered the eastern bank. The one that led back to their camp. Knives were aimed at their faces. The Scavengers' Zodiacs were abandoned, as were their dead. It took less than forty seconds for the enemy to escape with Drake's friends. It was several more minutes before Dallas managed to land them on the closest, western, bank.

No one spoke as they left the Zodiac behind and returned to the rapids.

They were in a hurry to find Mai, but leaving their friends in Scavenger hands wasn't an option.

They raced to Dahl and patted his face, shouting at the big Swede, trying to wake him up. Drake saw a bruise at his right temple. Finally, as the minutes stretched by, he allowed himself to drag the unconscious man to the river and dunk his head underwater.

Dahl woke spluttering.

Drake kept a straight face. "Nice nap?"

"What happened?"

"Get up. We'll explain as we walk."

They picked up the pace.

CHAPTER SIXTEEN

Mai waited for Luther to adjust another trap before moving on. This was the fourth in as many minutes and every time they stopped it cost them time. Luther had managed to rejig just one. They had also been forced to cross another gap, this one only three feet in width. An easy jump, but the way Dino and Karin did it showed they were flagging.

Mai asked Luther to wait behind at the entrance to a small cave to determine how far behind their pursuers were, and pressed on. Ten minutes later, Luther returned. The news wasn't good.

"Eight minutes max," he said.

Mai waited until everyone took on water, and ate chocolate and energy bars. It wasn't lasting nutrition, but it was all they had. They rested for less than a minute. More traps presented themselves ahead—all basic, makeshift snares and tricks designed to maim or break bones. Mai narrowly missed stepping in an ankle loop, which would have pulled her up and dashed her against the side of the tunnel. Luther noticed a jumble of rocks that covered a primed grenade. He wasted no time rescuing the grenade from its rocky nest and clipping it to his belt.

Ahead, Mai saw the biggest problem yet.

"Help me," she said and sprang forward. They'd encountered a rockslide just around a sharp corner where the passage widened a few feet. Large boulders blocked the way forward.

"This isn't random," Dino said as he rolled stone after stone to the side.

Mai agreed and again asked Luther to watch their backs. She worked fast, handing each rock off to Karin, but soon Luther was back.

"They're coming," he whispered. "Just behind me."

Mai didn't hesitate, just spun away from the rock she was working on, pulled out her knife and stalked to the blind corner.

"Keep working," she hissed when Karin and Dino turned to her. "It's our only way out of here."

The enemy came. She confronted them at the narrowest point. When the first man darted into sight, she grabbed his wrist and forced his gun barrel upward. He fired reflexively. Bullets strafed the roof. Mai leaned in and rammed the knife into his chest, cursing when it hit a stab vest. The man reeled, grunting in pain. She slipped through a small gap, now behind him, using the semi-dark to her advantage. Now she faced another man who looked shocked to see her face. She slashed his bicep and kicked out at his rifle, sending it clattering to the floor.

Quickly then, she stabbed the first where his vest didn't reach.

It was intense, close-quarter battle. The passage was only wide enough to accommodate one and a half people. The man whose bicep she'd slashed turned, fists smashing down at her. She ducked under, let him hit the rock wall, came up and flicked her blade at another merc. Blood splashed across his face. She could see Valance three rows distant, and behind him, the four civilians.

Maybe if she could take the trophy hunters out, the mercs might realize they had nothing to fight for and leave.

The man at her back tried to encircle her throat with a tattooed arm. She spun lightly and broke it, forcing him into his own men. Upsetting the entire group's balance, she found some space, ran and kicked out with both feet, breaking one man's ribs and sending two others tumbling.

Then, Luther was close. "My turn," he breathed. "You can't do it all."

She nodded and spun away. Luther charged into battle, giving their enemy a new challenge. Far from the deft, precise killing machine that was Mai Kitano, they now faced the blunt, old-fashioned warrior. Luther hit them like a landslide.

Mai ran back to Karin and Dino. They glanced once at the blood spattered across her face and chest and nodded.

"Good work."

The rock pile had thinned nicely during the minute or so she'd been fighting. A three-foot gap was evident. Mai got to work, helping and resting at the same time. When she'd ticked another minute off in her head she returned to Luther.

"Shout out when you're done," she told Karin.

Luther was in the thick of it. A man lay crushed against the left rock wall, another was being trampled underfoot. Luther lifted a third by the collar of his jacket and threw him back amongst his comrades.

"I'll take over," Mai said.

They fought in hard, brutal silence, first Mai and then Luther, as Karin and Dino cleared the way. It was bloody and mean. It was sheer hell. The claustrophobic nearness of it all. The surrounding rock below and above as well as to the side. The dancing, flame-lit shadows. The bodies at their feet hampered all movement. Mai figured there were ten mercs left alive, plus Valance. Several others were bruised or carrying injuries including broken bones. If they survived this battle Mai knew they'd vastly improved their chances of leaving the cave network alive.

Twice, Mai tried to reach down and collect a gun. Both times the risk wasn't worth it, as she took major blows and almost passed out. After that, she concentrated on debilitating her enemy, keeping hold of the knife, and listening out for Karin's shout.

Finally, it came. Luther was at her side a second later. This would be the toughest part.

"Time to get the hell outta here," he said.

She focused on keeping their enemy at bay, making sure they couldn't fire shots in the enclosed space. "Plan?"

"Yeah, we definitely need one."

Then Valance shouted from further down the tunnel: "You think you won? Think again. You have no idea what's up ahead."

Mai ignored him, still struggling.

"I almost hope you escape the caves," Valance sneered. "To see what awaits on the mountain."

Luther attacked, smashing into the lead merc and sending him flying back among his colleagues. Mai skipped to the side as he passed by, then turned and ran. The gap had been widened to about five feet ahead. Dino and Karin were already through.

"Ready?" she cried.

"We got it."

She scrambled through, spine raked by the edge of a sharp rock, exposed flesh cut and bleeding as she wriggled hard. Within a few seconds, Luther hit the gap and bellowed as he got stuck.

There wasn't time!

The chasing pack would be on him any second. She reached out, grabbed his right wrist and pulled. Dino grabbed the left. Luther fought his way forward, ripping his T-shirt and trousers. With a final heave he was through.

The rock wall collapsed at his back, more boulders tumbling down. Luther grunted in pain as he rose, staring down at himself.

"Looks like I fought a pair of friggin' lions."

Mai patted his shoulder. "Stop crying about it, baby. I've seen men look worse after an hour with Alicia."

Luther gingerly touched a cut, a gesture that looked quite odd coming from the large warrior.

Dino stared. "I'd offer you my jacket," he said. "But no way is it gonna fit."

They heard activity on the other side of the rock pile.

"Best start moving," Luther said.

Mai ignored the aches and pains from bruises, cuts and impact wounds. She thought about the future and started forward. She thought about fresh air, about freedom, about seeing their friends once more.

The sight of Luther standing there had jolted her, mostly because her first thought had been: *Whoa, if he looks that good in a ripped T-shirt, I wonder how he looks with no clothes on?*

If they survived all this, she vowed to find out.

CHAPTER SEVENTEEN

The Devil was rarely shocked these days but, right now, he barely believed his eyes. His jaw worked but no sound came out. Mostly in darkness he clenched his fists, tensed his body, and bared his teeth.

The timer on the mini-nuke read: *12:00*. Twelve hours.

By the Devil's reckoning it should read twenty-three.

He thinks he can do this to me? To me! Kovalenko thinks he can destroy me? My island? You don't kill the Devil so easily, you little Russian fuck!

Desperate for retribution, but intelligent enough to focus and set his priorities straight, the Devil took stock of his situation. Vengeance would come, it would visit the Blood King like a killer tsunami. For now, though, he considered the evacuation stages of his plan. This new development changed very little apart from escalating timings.

Anger chewed through his gut. *I helped the little upstart. I gave him shelter. The entire world is hunting him down.*

Well now, it was the world and the Devil. There would be a reckoning for this betrayal. The Devil considered his small army of paid mercenaries and the island itself. He considered the clans, the prisoners inside the compound. Plans came to him like wasps around ice cream.

But which works best for me?

The answer came, and it was good. It filled the Devil with warmth and light, made both sides of his harsh mouth draw up. It was the closest thing to a warm tingle he ever remembered having.

Turning, leaving the bomb to its dark and nefarious countdown, he retraced his steps and left the building, emerging into the mid-morning light. For a moment he let his eyes adjust, still thinking, still refining his plan. The first things he saw as he left the cover of the inner buildings were Kovalenko's compounds. Here, prisoners were kept. True, the man had paid handsomely to store them here but now everything had changed. The Devil wondered if he should simply order them all shot.

He had become used to the slaves, to their subservience and fear. But he didn't depend on them. He didn't need them. And the other prisoners? He didn't know who most of them were. Wives Kovalenko needed to help coerce husbands. In what the Devil thought was a perverse twist, some of these captives dated back to the old Blood King. They'd been here that long; the authorities had either given up or not been pushed hard enough by relatives to search for them. If you don't shout up you're just another face in a very large crowd.

His gaze switched to the ocean, counting the vessels at anchor. He had more than enough, but more people meant more hardship, more headaches and more mouths to feed.

The original idea might be best.

They've been captives for so long. Wait until we're ready and then tell them they're free. Let them out of their cages. That should give them at least an hour to enjoy the island before it explodes.

Perfect.

The Devil loved it, but there were other problems. Without a lieutenant to relay his orders, the Devil would have to do everything himself. In truth, this menial task wasn't all bad. He preferred total control. Nothing left to chance or the whims of others. In any case there was something he could use to spread the word.

This island had a tannoy system. Something most islands in the Pacific employed to warn of hurricanes, tsunamis, typhoons and the like. He reminded himself that this was his island. The clans out there and the mercenaries in the castle continued to exist at his whim. The Blood King's betrayal threw a new viewpoint into the mix. The Devil made a U-turn in his thinking, purely because it was the opposite of what Kovalenko wanted.

He wasn't about to let the clansmen die in nuclear fire.

Smiling, he entered the block and mortar hut that housed the tannoy system. Wiping dust from the controls and throwing the rickety chair to the side, he raised the mic to his lips and watched out of the ocean-facing window.

"Stop what you are doing," he said. "And listen."

Almost everyone he could see halted or turned their faces toward the castle. Mercs paused with boxes in their hands. Others stopped their conversation. Even the slaves looked up in wonder. Of course, most people didn't know there was a tannoy system that covered almost the entire island.

He repeated the sentences, making sure he had everyone's attention. Then, choosing his words carefully, he laid out his plan.

"Luka Kovalenko—the so-called new Blood King—has just sailed away. It seems he left something behind. A nuclear bomb . . ." The Devil paused to let that sink in. "A nuclear bomb that can't be disarmed. This bomb will detonate in twelve hours, ten less than he told us. I say now—get your things, get everyone together and get away from this island. Quickly. Find the mainland and then—everyone—find a way to kill Luka Kovalenko. Your time on my island is finished."

Nodding to himself, the Devil put the speaker down, but then decided to repeat himself. Recalling the state of mind of some of the islanders, it was probably for the best. He checked the compound and the docks to see how his news had been received.

It could have been worse, he guessed. Boxes of supplies had been dropped. Some men were already running for the ships, idiots that didn't listen to all the information. Armed mercenaries were jostling each other along the docks. Some were fighting. The slaves were on their knees, having fought so hard to survive all these years only to find their struggles came down to this fateful day.

Hopefully the islanders would be preparing. The Marauders and the Creepers, the Hunters and even the horrifying Scavengers would make ready to set sail. Every last one of them intent on hunting down Kovalenko.

It made for a fine vision.

The Devil had lived here so long he'd forgotten what it was like to coexist with civilians. If Kovalenko hadn't double-crossed him he'd have let the island explode purely because the clans had taken most of it, confining him to his castle.

But I won't be confined. Not anymore.

The best plans are fluid, subject to constant refinement. The island evacuation had always had many facets, several nuances, and every one of these now came into play.

Of course, his yacht was already prepped. Everything he needed was on board. All that it required to set sail was the Devil himself. He wondered briefly about Valance, leading his mercs through the catacombs in pursuit of the warriors. The only issue there was the civilians he'd brought along—they might be missed. Still, the Devil had their home details and could check. He wondered then about the genetic

monsters that lived on top of the mountains.
The banes of my existence. Good riddance.
Twelve hours. What can I do in that time?
There was no rush. The castle's systems were still up and running. Let the mercs fight if they wanted to, let them worsen their own chances of leaving here alive. The brightest would figure it out, which was all that he wanted. Maybe some of the slaves too would find a way to escape.

Let them. It didn't matter anymore.

What did matter was vengeance. The kind only a man like the Devil could deal. A very special kind.

That would come later. For now, he returned to his communications room and updated himself on how the DC scenario was playing out. First, he spent several serious minutes deciding whether to cancel the entire op—it was at Kovalenko's behest after all. Deciding he should, he picked up the phone to call his men off.

Then he paused.

Why? he thought. *You're enjoying it. You've put days of work into it. The whole thing's paid for. Wouldn't you like to see how it all plays out, despite Kovalenko?*

The answer was yes.

So when they picked up the call his words were: "Tell me where we are."

CHAPTER EIGHTEEN

Drake ran hard in the tracks of the Scavengers. Alicia and Dahl hurried along to the left, with Kenzie and Dallas to the right. It wasn't difficult to follow their enemies' footsteps; the problem was scanning the terrain for concealed killers.

After five minutes though, they were all forced to stop.

A man they assumed was the Devil made a stunning tannoy announcement. His voice filled the air, radiating from dozens of concealed speakers. Drake guessed it was like an old air-raid warning system, something installed when the place had first been inhabited.

The team exchanged glances.

"Do we believe this?" Dallas asked.

"Set your watches," Drake said. "Twelve hours. And we believe it unless we see otherwise."

"It could help," Kenzie pointed out. "By getting the clans out of our way."

Drake scanned the earth for signs of passage. "Maybe. This Devil guy seems to think everyone will follow his orders. I can't see that happening."

"But they have to leave the island."

Drake leapt over a fallen tree and started up an earthy slope. "No, they don't," he said. "And even if they do, twelve hours is a long time. Most of the islanders have subsisted for years. It's all they know. Their entire way of life. Nuclear bomb or not, it'll be a tough decision."

Kenzie looked unconvinced, but Drake knew she wasn't seeing through the eyes of a local. She couldn't. They came to a rise and paused for a moment to catch their breath and get their bearings.

"Scavengers' camp is that way." Dahl pointed to the west. "A solid half-hour walk."

"Can't see them," Dallas added.

Drake looked over the rolling green hills all the way to the black rock mountains they'd climbed hours earlier. Nothing moved out there, but he imagined there were several dozen people preparing to enact their leader's escape plan. What that was likely to be, Drake didn't want to know.

Once more, his team had been torn apart. Mai and the others abducted and forced to walk the Devil's catacombs. Hayden and the others taken by a band of wild animals, intent on slaughter. The very idea of it hurt his brain and his heart.

"We need intel," he said. "Use the drone."

For once, Dahl agreed. They wasted no time unpacking it and switching it on. As they worked, Alicia checked again for a phone signal but whatever device the Devil was using to jam the signals was still fully operative. Soon, Dahl was holding the drone's controller close and focusing on its buttons.

The drone lifted into the air, a low buzzing sound marking its passage.

"You used one of these before?" Dallas asked.

"Not really," Dahl admitted. "You?"

"I have a Mavic at home. Use it all the time."

Dahl handed the controls over. "Be my guest, but don't crash it."

Drake crouched down to study a monitor. The drone would send a video feed of everything it saw as it flew over the island. "Start with the Scavengers," he said. "And then a quick tour of the whole island."

"No problem."

They crowded around the monitor. A flat field then a

rolling hill came into view as the drone rose into the sky. Then the view from the top of their hill as it started forward, followed by the landscape beneath it as it started to fly. Empty, green and brown sloping fields spread out below.

"To the right," Dahl said. "Follow the straight path toward their camp."

Dallas altered the course. Two minutes later the monitor showed figures below, running across the open fields. Drake counted ten Scavengers. He saw Hayden, Kinimaka and Molokai being forced to walk in their midst. Even as they watched, Hayden stumbled and was dragged on her knees until she found a way to stand. Molokai smashed two enemies aside, ready to fight, but was confronted by four more, all brandishing handguns. One man appeared to fire a bullet, but Molokai didn't fold. Maybe it had been a warning shot.

Dallas flew the drone past the group before they spotted it, moving on to their camp. The few remaining Scavengers were emptying out their lean-tos and makeshift holes, cutting down any prisoners that were tied to stakes and making sure they were dead. One of the men looked up as the drone flew over, took out his gun and fired. The bullet missed but the warning remained. These men remembered full well what a drone could do.

Drake saw a few others rounding up supplies. Clearly, they were getting ready to move. Dallas sent the drone flying further toward the western horizon, coming around the mountain and across the wilderness where the Hunters held sway. Finally, he made a pass over the castle and then by the mountain, swinging around and heading back to base.

Drake took it all in. The Marauders were gathered

together, sitting on rocks and talking. Every single man looked up as the drone crossed over, but nobody moved. Drake saw what looked like cave dwellings behind them, their entrances covered by doors hewn from tree trunks, their meeting place surrounded by effigies, piles of stone, and stores of food and water. One of the men appeared to be talking into a long-range radio.

Beyond them, he saw the ocean spread out from horizon to horizon and then the wilderness on the island's southeastern corner. This was where the Hunters lived. It wasn't long before he glimpsed them. Most were bare chested and heavily bearded. They carried bows and arrows in addition to guns and knives. They too were gathered together, standing before a big man that appeared to be their leader. Many were gesticulating wildly. The land around them was indeed barren, divested of most of its color and vibrancy. It appeared almost blighted, as if the Devil had carried out an experiment upon it. Drake wondered what they ate but then saw a coarse staircase cut into the cliffs leading down to the sea. Two men were trudging up it even now, carrying sacks full of fish.

Onward swept the drone, minutes passing in flight as it flew over rugged knolls and jagged peaks, across dales where yellow grass grew, and by a single sparkling stream. Soon it reached the castle, making Drake and the others sit forward. Whatever they learned here could prove vital.

"Man," Alicia grunted. "That's a bloody army."

Drake didn't like the look of it either. Dozens of men thronged the dock area and a compound that sat outside the castle walls on the beach. Dallas slowed the drone to its most leisurely speed. The mercs appeared to be arguing, maybe even fighting. Several ships and yachts sat in the harbor. Drake saw two superyachts and wondered if one might belong to Kovalenko.

No, the tannoy announcement said he'd departed.

Someone else's then. He saw bamboo-walled jail cells and what appeared to be captives. The castle main buildings were strong and sturdy, the central keep higher than the others. The walls were manned by a dozen men with weapons, all staring out at their surroundings.

"They're not guarding the mountain," Kenzie said.

"Looks too high to abseil down," Dahl said, "with the equipment we have."

Irregular black rock soared high above the castle, its face navigable but dangerous. Drake agreed with Dahl. If they had the time and the right equipment the descent was doable. As they were . . . it was out of the question. But first he needed to concentrate on the mountain. As the drone flew over the top he watched but saw nothing unusual.

Shrubbery. Boulders. A wide plateau. A rock feature that could well lead down to the catacombs. Toward the south it sloped into the sea, its slopes giving way to thick stands of trees, impenetrable ground cover and more jagged rock. There wasn't even a beach. The mountain joined the sea, its lowest slopes forever lashed by the elements.

"Isn't that where the genetic experiments live?" Kenzie studied the summit.

"What . . . you think they're gonna be lined up and waving?" Alicia looked at her.

"I wish Mai was there," Drake said. "Waving."

The drone completed its tour of the island, flying back to them. Drake thought it had been an informative flight. Dallas packed it away as the others prepared to chase down the Scavengers.

"We know exactly where they are," Dahl said. "Everyone ready?"

They started forward, moving faster now that they knew

the landscape and were 95 percent sure nobody was lying in wait for them. It was a straight run to the Scavenger camp.

Drake jogged with Dallas and Kenzie just ahead. Of course, they knew nothing about the newcomer but he'd proven useful in saving the President and had stood by them all the way to Devil's Island. They'd dig down to the nitty gritty later.

"Is this what it's always like?" Dallas was asking. "With SPEAR?"

"Not exactly," Kenzie said. "But there's always death, danger and action."

"Is that why you quit?"

"No. I wanted to return to the wrong side of the law."

Drake could tell Dallas didn't quite believe her. "But you came back to help them."

"I returned to help *me*," Kenzie snapped. "Stop asking dumb questions."

"And what happens next?" Dallas asked a question Drake was interested in hearing the answer to. "Back to interviewing mercs for a new relic smuggling team?"

"Well, apparently, Hayden has a new proposal." Kenzie sighed deeply as she ran. "I guess I'll have to hear her out first."

"Maybe I'll stick with you," Dallas said.

"Maybe I'll let you."

"You're not that alluring, you know."

"You're kidding?" Kenzie looked across at him. "If I wanted to I'd have you eating out of my hands."

"Really?" Dallas's reply was a little too fast and forced. "I doubt that."

Suddenly, ahead, Dahl stopped. He turned to face them. "I don't think we can do this," he said.

Drake skidded to a halt. "What are you talking about?"

"The timing's too tight," Dahl said. "I've been running it through my brain. We'll lose hours saving Hayden and the others. Then hours to reach the mountain. After that we need to find Mai, save those captives and find a way off the island before the nuke blows."

Drake narrowed his eyes. "We don't have time."

Dahl nodded. "So, what are we gonna do?"

Desperation clawed inside his stomach. There was only one choice, and nobody was going to like it.

CHAPTER NINETEEN

Pursuit came fast.

To Mai it felt deliberate. Up until now their pursuers had moved at a similar pace but now she heard and sensed an urgency. Were they trying to close the gap?

They couldn't be nearing the exit so why would they do that now? When she voiced her concern to Luther he looked at her and uttered one word: "Trap."

It happened fast. One minute they were negotiating the dark, roughhewn tunnels, the next they had emerged into a vast cavern that needed no artificial light. Mai stumbled, brain shocked as the walls vanished to left and right. Heat and light hit her at the same time, making her throw her arms in front of her face.

"Don't stop." Luther propelled her forward. "They're less than a minute behind."

It looked bad. Mai had been in some dangerous scrapes through the years—from Tokyo Coscon to Washington DC—but this could well be the worst. Their path ended about twenty feet ahead where a lava pit dissected the cave. The glow shining up from it was hellish and hot. Gobbets of lava exploded from below, some shooting straight up into the air whilst others came diagonally, landing on the cave floor.

The gap was twelve feet wide. A single plank of solid wood was the only way across. Mai guessed it measured about two feet in width.

The plank's underside was hit by a lava-bomb even as she watched. Then, a harsh blast flew up and splatted the ceiling, before raining down fire, dripping like melting glass. Within seconds she had assessed the whole cave.

"There's only one way to go." Luther stalked forward, making sure his backpack was secure.

"We could stop and fight," Dino said. "It worked last time."

Mai wiped sweat from her forehead. "But at some point, we'll still have to cross that." She pointed at the plank. "Better now so that at least some of us survive."

Karin eyes opened wide at her words, as if she'd just realized how deadly this underground pursuit was. Mai placed a hand on her arm. "We're not all gonna make it," the Japanese woman said softly. "I'm sorry."

Luther was at the edge of the lava pit, looking down. Mai joined him, Dino and Karin at her side. It was a white-hot mess below. Fire bubbled, spat and boiled. A shimmering wall of heat dried out the water in their eyes.

"You first." Luther nodded at Karin. "Then Mai, Dino and me. Move."

Mai knew he wasn't being solicitous. It was simply the best order to cross, keeping at least one experienced member of the team with a younger one. And she was nimbler, able to cross faster. If Luther went first he'd slow the whole group down.

But crossing was a whole new matter. Without the spitting lava and a long drop it would have been simple. Karin held her arms out for balance and put one foot in front of the other, teetering at first. She stared ahead but down, keeping the plank at the forefront of her vision. It was the next gout of flame she was waiting for—they all were.

Their pursuers arrived.

Karin was halfway across the plank. Mai was ready to

start over. Luther was covering them all, standing in the center of the cave. Mai saw four of the ten remaining mercs surge out of the tunnel, followed by Valance and the four rich civilians, and then more mercs. Everyone came to a sudden halt.

Valance laughed. "Here we go," he said. "What did I tell you?"

All four civilians chortled along with him, taking in the shocking sight that was the lava cave. The mercs lowered their weapons and fanned out in front of Luther. Karin picked up the pace. Mai stepped out onto the plank behind her.

"Take your pick." Valance indicated them. "I'd recommend knocking one of them into the lava. It's great sport."

The civilian trophy hunters unstrapped rifles from their shoulders and dropped to one knee. Karin was five feet from the other side when a lava bomb exploded. Fire shot past her left shoulder, emanating intense heat. Karin flinched away, lost her footing on the plank and toppled.

She fell toward the fire pit. One of the trophy hunters cheered.

Somehow, she hooked a knee over the plank and landed on her inner thigh, crying out with pain but managing to hang on. She hooked her hands over the nearby ledge and crawled the last few feet, rolling to safety. Mai ignored the lava burst, speeding up. Dino stepped out behind her.

Luther used his bulk to block their enemies aim.

"Remove him," Valance told his men.

Mai felt her heart lurch. It felt like someone had dosed her with ice water. Running forward across the narrow plank, she looked back. At that moment a spear of fire shot across the plank, landing right before her, sizzling on the hard wood and making it burn. Dino yelled out a warning. Mai jumped headlong, above the rock plank and the fire that dripped off it, trusting to balance and aim to save her life. She came down three feet further along, still running, sure-footedly hitting the middle of the length of wood.

Behind her, Dino pulled up.

"Luther! Move!"

Mai turned to see four mercs rushing the big warrior. Valance hadn't meant "kill him" then. "Remove him" was a literal term. Luther shrugged the first two off without giving ground, sending them sprawling left and right. The third hit head on, shoulders down, forcing Luther backward even though he planted both heels in the ground. Luther grabbed hold of the man's shoulders and heaved him away.

Mai jumped to safety. The trophy hunters had sighted their rifles on Dino and were ready. The first fired. His bullet snagged Dino's left shoulder and spun him around. Crying out in pain he fell right off the path.

Mai jumped, catching his body round the middle a second before he fell, and clamping hold. His weight dragged her down. She couldn't hold on. Karin grabbed her and, exposed, the two women held on to Dino. Mai reached up to grip the ledge once more. Dino was crying out but not from the pain where the bullet had nicked him. It was from the heat washing over his feet and legs. Mai heard the crack of another bullet, saw it impact close to where her right hand gripped the ledge.

She heard a chorus of cheers and boos, one man boasting about how close he'd gotten, the others berating him for missing. Another shot rang out and glanced off the rock near Karin's head. There was another bout of yelling and booing.

Luther tackled the fourth attacker, spinning around with

the man in a bear hug, letting him go close to the edge of the pit. There was a terrified yell as the merc realized his fate. Unable to save himself he plummeted over the edge and was incinerated below. Luther turned to another man that was climbing to his feet, very close to that same ledge. He ran and then jumped with both boots facing forward, smashing the man in the chest and sending him tumbling into the lava pit.

Valance yelled out in anger. "Shoot that bastard's legs out!"

Luther was already taking precautions. He grabbed one of the men he'd felled earlier and swiveled so the man was between him and his enemy. The first bullet took his human shield in the chest, the second in the stomach, both shots non-fatal due to hitting body armor. Luther held on tight, retreating toward the rock plank.

Mai channeled every ounce of energy into one huge heave. Karin held on tight. Her own body fell back to safety. She didn't let up, dragging Dino over as well. One more bullet came close, impacting between Dino's dangling legs.

"Stop playing and shoot them!" Valance yelled.

The four Great White Hunters looked miffed at having their fun stopped, one of them giving the head merc the finger. Mai was torn between wanting to help Luther and taking Karin and Dino out of the cave and into the exit tunnel.

But there was no question here. Karin and Dino were grown adults, trained soldiers, and should stand or die on their own merit. Pointing out the escape tunnel, she spun back to Luther.

The big man was struggling, being forced to walk backward whilst being shot at. Required to keep the same position, he couldn't check back to find the plank. Also, he was bigger than the man he was using as a shield. It wouldn't be long before a bullet found him.

Mai didn't hesitate. She ran out across the fire pit once more, using the trophy hunters' gleeful rebelliousness to gain the time she needed, and pressed her back to Luther's.

"Stay with me and maintain contact," she said. "Come with me."

Back to back, she led Luther across the narrow shelf of rock, keeping her hands at his sides. She was covered by his bulk and that of the mercenary he dragged along. She felt bullets impact; the shuddering of the man; the grunting of Luther; the man's great strength as he fought against the blows and held on to his enemy at the same time. It was deadly at first, stepping out over the lava pit. The merc struggled; his feet slipped and missed and swung out over heated air.

But after several hairy seconds their shield stopped struggling, realizing that if they fell—he would too.

Together then, they negotiated the shelf. The civilians peppered them with bullets, hitting the merc's legs before Valance could say otherwise—if he was even going to—making him scream in pain and sag helplessly.

Luther somehow held on, dragging him along. Mai kept them straight with her body, making sure Luther's spine stayed dead center with hers.

Two thirds of the way across, Valance came to a decision. "After them!"

Mai fought the urge to run. They stayed together until they reached the end of the plank and jumped to safety. By then, the mercs were halfway across. Luther waited until they came close and then threw his hapless captive at them.

Mai ran. Luther followed. Shots rang out. Bullets skimmed the walls. The man Luther had thrown struck the first runner dead center. Both men flew down into the lava pit. The others came to an abrupt stop, falling to their knees to keep their balance.

Mai used the distraction to reach the exit tunnel. Luther was a step behind.

"Thanks," he said.

"You owe me again."

"Pay me back by surviving."

"Y'know, I think I might just do that."

Following Karin and Dino, they hurried down another tunnel; disgusted, angry shouts coming from Valance at their backs.

CHAPTER TWENTY

The Devil paced, running two scenarios though his head and trying to decide which one should take precedence. He was ensconced in his surveillance room, surrounded by monitors and local feeds as well as the remote ones he was using to keep an eye on events transpiring in Washington DC.

The first scenario involved escaping the island and then organizing his new hideout in America. The second scenario entailed dealing with the Dahls.

The problem with the hideout was the time it would take. The Devil was looking at many months of organization, oversight and low-key operations to make it all come together. This put an emphasis on the second scenario, which would take just a few days.

But he didn't trust anyone. If he set the supply boat on a course for the United States, who was going to make sure it arrived?

No matter. He'd appoint a captain and threaten the man's loved ones. He knew the backstory of every mercenary who'd been on this island longer than a month. He had reams and reams of data stored away.

Based on that single thought, the Devil knew which scenario he preferred. He licked his lips. This was going to be fun.

A moment later he had the DC team on the line. "Report."

"We're stoking the locals. The parade crosses close to the

east of the city where crime is worst. We toyed with fuelling the hate crimes, drug use, cartels and the gun laws. We decided on the former. Honestly, it's not hard here. DC may be the HQ of the FBI and home to the President, but crime is happily prevalent."

"Can you bring it all together in time?"

"We're checking all angles. We're using social media to fool those most likely to commit hate crimes into thinking the parade will be loaded with the kind of people they hate. It's ridiculously easy."

The Devil nodded. It wasn't hard to sway a man surrounded by constant animosity and full of anger. The tricky part was in directing his fury to the right place.

"I'm coming to you," he said, forcing his voice to remain calm. "I want everything ready so that I can take charge at the end."

"You want the killing blow?"

"I do."

"On the wife or on all three?"

The Devil thought about it with cold detachment. Emotions were not his thing. "The wife, for sure. Let's see how the parade pans out, though. We may need to improvise."

"Our view too," his acolyte said. "Two days then."

The Devil was silent for a moment and then said: "Five Guys?"

"Ah," there was a respectful chuckle. "I forgot how much the Devil likes his Five Guys. A shame you can't get them flown to the island."

"That won't matter soon. I'll update you when we meet. For now, keep on top of the local enmity and make me proud."

"Yes, sir."

"One last thing. An update on the targets."

"Nothing much to tell. Johanna takes her kids to school, hits the gym and lunches before driving home. She tidies and watches a few documentaries before heading out to collect the girls later. Then, they either go to the mall, eat out and shop, or return home and cook. They take it in turns. After the kids go to bed, Johanna wastes an hour on social media before renting a movie. She's a fan of rom-coms. Probably hates action movies because it reminds her of the dangers her husband faces. She's usually in bed by eleven."

"That's a typical day for Johanna Dahl?"

"That's every day. It rarely differs."

"Except when she plans a big day out."

"Yes, sir. Just like the day of the parade."

The Devil signed off and took a long look around his surveillance room. This part of his life was nearly over. Soon, everything would change.

It was time to embrace a fantastic future.

In America.

The thought gave him goosebumps.

CHAPTER TWENTY ONE

Torsten Dahl took Dallas and Kenzie with him in pursuit of Hayden, Kinimaka and Molokai. They were stretched pretty thin. It was beyond risky. But nobody saw a better way. Mai would be heading to the top of the mountain. Did she even know about the monsters that made their lairs up there? And then there was Hayden's plight. They couldn't be left in the hands of the Scavengers. Not after the things Dahl had seen in their camp. But now they also faced the added complication with the nuke. The hours were ticking down.

The Devil was escaping. The Blood King had already left. SPEAR had come late to this party. It seemed they were here solely to mop up. Dahl raced through undergrowth, the rising warmth of the sun hot on his back. Sweat dripped from his brow and chin. Dallas ran to his right, Kenzie to his left. Nobody spoke. They hurried up a long, sharp slope and ran over the top, jogging down the incline. The Scavengers had left a wide trail. He guessed they were about twenty minutes ahead, maybe less. For the third time in as many minutes he checked his weapons.

Dahl wasn't used to being nervous. It was a combination of this island's inhabitants, their friends being in peril, and lack of proper rest. Truth be told, Dahl hadn't rested in months. He was a family man, a loyal man, and the distance between his wife and children had become a vast gulf, littered with traps. He couldn't span it. Months ago, Johanna and he had overcome their biggest problem. They had decided to stick together, try again. They took a holiday in Barbados and ended up fighting for their children's lives. It brought the real world home to their family, and all the bad things that could happen to good people. For a while they had been in a good place.

But Dahl's job was demanding. He knew it. He knew that one day, very soon, it would come down to the job or the family. Dahl couldn't continue to do both. Was there a compromise?

To start mending . . . you first had to try.

If the harsh sun beating down upon them wasn't enough, a steady drizzle began to fall. Dallas voiced his surprise, but Kenzie reminded him of the island's numerous climate zones. Dahl tried to stop the Israeli intruding on his personal thoughts.

"Keep your voices down," he snapped, more harshly than he'd intended.

Kenzie came up alongside him. "It's not wrong to feel attraction, Torsten. You haven't acted on it."

He wondered if it was so bloody obvious. "I worry that it's influencing my thoughts."

"You're a good man," Kenzie said. "Probably the best I've ever met. It's why . . . it's why I left."

"You left because I'm good?" Dahl leapt over a narrow stream.

Kenzie shrugged. "I hated to see you struggling."

"You made it all easier."

"I guess."

"And then you came back."

"Well, I didn't have much choice!"

Dahl held a hand up to show he'd been overly cynical. It wasn't fair to punish her for events outside her control. "It's not as simple as removing temptation." He gave her a smile. "It's about repairing something, and you don't know how it broke in the first place. Where do you start?"

"Being together, I guess." Kenzie shrugged, unsure.

Dahl shook his head. "That's all well and good," he said, ducking as they negotiated a stand of trees. "But being together solves nothing."

"So talk," Kenzie started to sound exasperated. "You normally don't have that problem!"

Dahl looked at her speculatively. "You're right," he said. "But with lifelong partners—it's harder than that."

"Why?"

"I have no bloody idea."

They slowed, aware that they had covered a good deal of ground. Dallas was slightly ahead, giving them space. They topped another rise.

Dahl flung himself down onto his stomach.

Ahead, hurrying along the lush lower seam of a fold in the land, was the Scavenger party. Ten men with varying weapons, all stripped to the waist and wearing an assortment of shorts, ripped pants and what appeared to be a loincloth in one example, scarred and ruthless, shouting aloud with anger and hatred, men turned into savages by their situation. In their midst, Hayden, Kinimaka and Molokai either walked or were dragged. The slightest stumble attracted heavy recompense. A let up in the pace wasn't allowed. Hayden was bleeding from the head and Kinimaka limped.

Dallas pointed ahead. "Their camp's right there."

Dahl swore. They hadn't caught up in time to catch their enemy in the open.

Kenzie grunted. "It could be for the better. They'll be less wary at camp. Might leave the prisoners alone for a bit."

"No," Dallas said. "They'll be busy packing their suitcases."

Dahl sighed at the weak attempt at humor. But it was true. The Scavengers would be making ready to leave the island. From what he could see though, very little seemed to be happening among the assortment of dwellings they called home.

"Let's get closer."

Fifteen cautious minutes later they were in a better position. The Scavengers' camp hadn't changed from what they'd seen earlier. What dwellings they could see in the wide depression were dirty and disorganized. Its inhabitants were walking to and fro or staring at the newcomers, asking questions. Some were infuriated—probably having lost friends. Some were brandishing knives and axes. Others sat around eating.

"No sense of urgency," Dallas said. "I wonder why."

"They're staying," Dahl said, barely able to believe his own words.

"They'd rather stay than change their lives," Kenzie said, "and return to the world. Or maybe they don't believe the Devil's announcement."

Dahl studied the scene. "Some of them are tooling up." He noticed a third of the men sorting through a weapons cache. "Maybe they're expecting an attack or . . ."

"From us?" Dallas interrupted.

"No, from other clans. Or maybe—they're attacking."

The big Swede gritted his teeth as Hayden, Kinimaka and Molokai were dragged to the center of the camp and forced to their knees. Men surrounded them. Three tied their hands behind their backs. Others circled them with knives, snarling.

"Are we ready?" Dahl asked.

"Fourteen enemies, total," Kenzie said. "We're ready."

"Get as close as you can before opening fire," Dahl said.

"Don't give them chance to exact retribution."

Hayden and the others were hauled to their feet, punched randomly, and then manhandled toward the thick, wooden stakes. A body still hung from the fourth, its flesh crusted with black blood and open wounds. All manner of weapons were trained on the captives, from a handgun to rifles to machetes and military knives. The more malicious among the Scavengers feigned attacks, laughing when their prisoners glared back without emotion.

Finally, Hayden and the others were properly tied. The Scavengers made a semi-circle around them staring, glaring, all with their backs to Dahl.

"It's now or never," the Swede said. "Let's roll."

CHAPTER TWENTY TWO

Drake and Alicia took a few minutes to get their bearings and then ran toward the base of the high mountain where Mai would emerge. They were still some way off, but it was imperative they reached it first, and not just to lend their aid. The clock was ticking, and Mai might not be aware. An unknown species of genetically modified animals roamed the top of it. The mercenaries that lived at the castle were gearing up to go.

They ran among trees, at first paying little heed to their surroundings until Drake heard a loud commotion to the right. They stopped and fell into the underbrush.

"The Creepers," Alicia whispered. "Remember—they live in the forest."

Drake cursed in silence. After leaving the rolling hills he'd been focused on the mountain and Mai. The sudden beginnings of a forest hadn't registered properly.

Luckily, the Creepers were busy.

Drake saw a large vehicle parked to the right, a black truck with an open-bed trailer. It was running, belching fumes, its diesel engine loud and probably why the Creepers remained unaware of his existence.

"Where the hell do they find diesel?" Alicia asked.

"Probably barter for it," Drake suggested. "They're the closest clan to the castle. Maybe they don't attack in return for fuel."

The truck was kitted out for war. Drake saw wicked spears fastened to the top of the cab, their deadly blades sticking out beyond the engine cover. He saw an archer strapped to the back of the cabin, quivers of arrows to left and right. He saw men arrayed in the back, weapons at the ready and several more crammed into the cab.

"They're going to war," Alicia said. "I wonder why."

"Could be protecting themselves on a journey to the shore," Drake shrugged, "looking for a boat."

"What's your count?"

"Fifteen."

"That leaves three elsewhere, if Tolley's count is right."

Drake glared at the surrounding trees as if they might reveal a face. "We can't hang around here, love. C'mon."

The Creepers were a tough-looking bunch. Strong and fit with rangy arms and legs covered by some type of hide. They appeared to have an abundance of weapons, though this included many made of wood and string, or possibly animal parts. Drake hadn't seen animals other than the islanders so far, but assumed there must be some. How else could all these people subsist? Not on fish alone, for sure.

He made ready to move. Alicia was staring behind them.

"What's wrong?"

"Nothing. Just hoping Hayden and the others are okay."

"They will be. Dahl's on the case. We have to help Mai."

Alicia shook her head wistfully. "Fucking Sprite. Always in trouble."

Drake recalled everything they'd seen through the mile-high eyes of the drone. "There's a huge mobilization happening right now all across this island," he said. "Including the castle and the docks. Our plane might not have time. It might be too dangerous. Alicia, we have to move and get Mai, and then think about how the hell we're gonna escape this place before the nuke goes off."

"Sure, you're the one spouting all the bollocks."

He shook his head wearily and started to sneak from one trunk to another. Together, they kept an eye on the sun-dappled branches above, watching for foes but seeing nothing. The Creepers, it seemed, were focused on their withdrawal. And who could blame them?

"Hell of a history here," Drake said as they crept along. "This island, I mean. Founded by the Devil, intentionally populated by the worst of the worst. I wonder if he originally meant to use them in some way?"

"You mean to impregnate each other?" Alicia looked horrified. "Shit, I hope not."

Drake scanned the horizon before sending her an annoyed glance. "Shit, not everything's about sex, Alicia."

"Stop talking like that. You're starting to sound mad-dog crazy."

Drake gave up. Clearly, she wasn't in the mood for chatter. "They turned on the Devil," he said. "He won't make that mistake twice. I wonder where he's going next?"

He saw interest creep across her face. "You know, that's a good point. This bloody Devil character has a shitload to answer for. We'd best not lose him too."

"And Kovalenko," Drake added, pausing behind a broad, coarse trunk.

"Just a rabid dog that needs putting down," Alicia said. "We'll catch up to him."

Ahead, the trees thinned out. Drake risked picking up the speed and soon they were leaving the forest behind, staring across a wide brown plain that led straight to the base of the mountain.

Drake unhooked his field glasses. "Nothing moving out there," he said. To the far right, at the edge of his field of vision, he could see the high castle walls. Ahead, the mountain dominated everything.

"Three p.m." Alicia checked her watch. "The daylight's running out."

Drake agreed and started off at pace. "Let's hope Mai, Luther and the others are there to greet us."

"Yeah," Alicia responded, but he knew by the tone of her voice that she expected much the opposite. *Something might be there to greet us,* Drake thought.

But it might not be human.

Shrugging it off, he put his head down and made a beeline for the mountain and all the horrors it harbored.

CHAPTER TWENTY THREE

Mai knew by the steep descent, by the way the tunnel was opening out, and by the fresh draft on her face, that they were nearing the top of the mountain. Even if she hadn't realized she'd have guessed from the increasingly angry shouts arising from their pursuers, that the end was coming.

They'd prepared something big for a terrible finale.

Mai was convinced of it, and told Luther, Karin and Dino. They hadn't come this far to fall at the last hurdle. To her count, there were eight mercs, Valance and the four trophy hunters left alive. The others agreed. With those numbers Mai expected the hunters to get in the way of the professionals. And she expected them to be nervous.

Luther still had the grenade he'd appropriated earlier. They all had their knives and the backpack. They moved at pace, still checking for traps but prioritizing speed. First Luther, then Dino, Mai and Karin led the way, taking their turns. It helped. At one bend in the tunnel they managed to heap several piles of rocks behind them. At another they rigged something that looked like a trap. It all bought them extra minutes.

The air grew sweeter. Luther, ahead, glanced back. "We still on for finishing that first date, Kitano?"

Mai shrugged off the tiredness. "Why? Is there a Denny's ahead?"

"You wanna date in a Denny's?"

"Not really, but you are an American."

"I can get hash browns and pancakes at Cooper's Hawk too."

She ignored the punishment her thighs and calves were receiving, just pushed on along the hard rock surface. "You've lost me there."

"I guess you'd call it a more upmarket diner. Me, I don't care either way."

"Me neither. Are we there yet?"

"Denny's? Yeah, it's just around the corner."

They plowed on, never slowing, hating the uphill run but happy to leave the underground tunnel system behind. Twice, they heard the rumbling mountain. Once more they saw a distant lava tube, its molten contents painting their surroundings a fiery red.

Karin and Dino ran at the back.

"You keeping up okay?" the Englishwoman asked her friend.

"Always at your heels, Blakey."

"Right where you belong."

"Ah, funny. Led me right into that one, didn't you?"

"It's always been easy."

They'd been bantering heavily for the last half hour. Mai saw it as a sign of nerves, of tiredness, but it was also part of their burgeoning affection. Clearly, there were certain disputes that needed resolving. Mai could think of only one way to solve them properly.

"When we get out of here," she shouted back. "You two should get a room."

"Yeah," Dino called back. "It'll be right beside Luther's and yours."

Mai grinned but didn't look back. Luther said nothing. In hardship, certain bonds were forged. It was hard to know if those bonds would survive once the action was over. Still . . . they could all have fun trying.

"Not far now," Luther breathed.

"I'm sure there will be one last trap at the very least," Mai said. "Get ready for it."

"Can't wait," Luther said, "because then, we're free."

"Don't forget the nuke."

The tunnel meandered up and up, the ceiling sometimes scraping their heads and, at others, vanishing into unknown heights. The fresh breeze petered out and then swept by in gusts. Their limbs ached. The pursuit continued and grew closer.

Mai wondered about Drake, about what had happened back in Paris and if the SPEAR team were on their tracks or maybe even decimated. The last she'd seen them had been on the slopes of a Parisian train track after they saved the President and let Luka Kovalenko walk free.

Seemed an awful long time ago now.

But she knew, if he was alive, Drake would be risking everything to save them.

It gave her an uplift, a new surge of hope. It didn't matter what had happened to their relationship—their friendship would always be as strong as mountains.

She stopped in mid-stride, horrified.

Stunned.

"This is it," she could barely form the whispered words. "The final trap. Oh, it's so much worse than I imagined."

Clearly, it was the last cavern. They could even see their exit. Luther joined her and then Karin and Dino stopped short to her left. Not a word passed among them as they took it all in.

Ahead, a wide, high cavern opened out. It was well-lit by many flickering torches set into the walls at varying heights. Ledges and outcroppings ran all the way to the top, maybe a hundred feet—where a wide hole showed a patch of sky, sunlight, and their way to freedom.

Between them and the walls lay hundreds and hundreds of bodies. Some in a state of decay. Some reduced to skeletons. Some fresh, as if just thrown down here yesterday. It was a mass grave, a body pit, and it stank of decomposition, death and blood. Flies buzzed over moldering corpses. Mai held her hand up to her nose and mouth as she stepped forward. The daylight up top was such a beautiful sight, marred by so much corruption.

"What is all this?" Karin asked, shaken and upset.

"Looks like they don't use graves," Luther said. "Probably mercs that die on the island. And there was some chatter of genetic experiments using the top of this mountain." He looked up. "I think this is where they dump their prey."

"What makes you say that?" Dino asked.

Luther pointed to several bodies. Mai stared then wished she hadn't. Large chunks had been taken from their arms, legs and stomachs.

"Are those . . . teeth marks?" Dino stared from the bodies to the hole in the roof. "What the hell is up there?"

"If we're lucky . . ." Luther nodded back down the passageway. "We'll find out. They're almost upon us."

"We can't climb," Karin said. "They'll pick us off easily. What do we do?"

Mai surveyed the sickening floor and set her face hard. "We fight."

It was thirty feet to the nearest rock wall. Mai fought down the revulsion and ran ahead, making an example. She managed to close her mind off and then pulled two comparatively fresh bodies over her own. She wriggled around to get the best view of the cavern's entrance, saw Luther and the others copying her.

She waited, knife in hand, ready to spring up when the best chance presented itself.

Three minutes passed. She fought down revulsion, closed her mind to the putrefying stench. The pursuit came closer and closer, the mercs as vocal as if they were taking a stroll through town. Mai waited patiently, clearing her mind. The next few minutes would decide if they left this place alive or joined the unlucky corpses on the floor.

A gentle breeze blew. She could even hear the calming noises of birds drifting down from above. A figure crossed her vision and then another. Four wary mercs entered the large cavern, betraying no surprise at the grisly sight that encountered their eyes. Carefully, they spread out. Valance came next and then the trophy hunters, closely followed by four more mercs. First, they scanned the walls and the darker corners and then looked all the way up to the top of the cavern.

"They got out?" one said incredulously. "Shit."

"You gotta be kidding me!" one of the trophy hunters snapped, wiping runnels of sweat from his brow. "All this frickin' way and the bastards escape? I want my fucking money back."

The other trophy hunters looked equally annoyed. Valance was staring with an odd expression on his face . . . almost as if he didn't quite believe what he was seeing. Mai knew that he'd soon make the inevitable connection.

She waited as long as she dared for the nearest merc to drift closer.

One, two . . .

Mai sprang to her feet, bringing the body with her. The merc flinched away. She took advantage, hurling the body in his direction and following it. She reached him at the same time as it did, springing around with her knife and slashing at his gun arm. The blade cut through his bicep, making him scream and stagger back. She grabbed his upper body, still holding the knife, and kept it between her and the other mercs.

It was an art, this kind of fighting.

Causing further distraction, the other three rose and attacked. The trophy hunters raised their guns and fired without aiming. Bullets flew in all directions, narrowly missing the fighting mercenaries. Luther hurled a corpse onto an opponent, bearing him to the ground, and then tackled another. Karin and Dino engaged others.

Together, they fought across the cavern floor.

Mai took the fight to their opponents, elbowing her merc in the face and then stabbing him through the ribs. She kept him upright, felt a bullet smash into his vest. By now she was right next to the shooter. She slipped around, grabbed his gun arm and broke it. He didn't flinch, just came at her with a knife. Mai stumbled over one of the bodies, fell to one knee. The man swiped down at her, but she moved in and heaved him over her head.

He landed heavily, crashing through a bleach-boned skeleton.

Valance had backed away, letting the trophy hunters step forward. Mai noticed Valance signal two of the mercs to remain at the back of the cavern alongside him. Karin and Dino matched their own opponents in skill but were about to become outnumbered. Luther saw it. Looping his massive right arm around one man's neck, he dragged them both into the fray that surrounded Karin.

A blow to someone's nose stopped them in their tracks. A kick to the groin sent another to the floor. Karin fell to one knee as a mercenary battered her head with two hands. But she still had the knife. She thrust it up into his lower stomach, left it there and dived away. He fell into the space she'd vacated.

By now Luther had strangled his man into unconsciousness. He let the man drop and then flung his own knife end over end through the air. It slammed point first into the right eye of a trophy hunter. The man died instantly, never knowing what hit him.

The other three hunters balked, not turning their weapons on the big man as they should do. Valance screamed at them. Mai stepped on the neck of the man she'd thrown and heard cartilage crack. She flung her own knife at one of the hunters; saw it glance off his gun where the sights were, making him drop it and fall to one knee.

She ran across a floor crammed with bodies. She stepped on bones and through chest cavities. She skidded as her right foot came down on someone's head and slid off. She fell to the left.

Karin ducked behind two piled up bodies. One crawled with maggots, the other was covered in flies. She tried to stop herself from heaving. A bullet smashed into the dead flesh that protected her. She was trapped, unarmed; one of the three remaining trophy hunters had singled her out to die.

Dino fought and kicked his own adversary. What the Italian-American had in skill, he lacked in strength, his light frame working against him in pitched battle. The merc he fought was big and well protected. Every blow Dino landed struck hard armor. His knife was trapped between their bodies.

The merc had fought to bring his gun up and now the barrel was slowly turning toward Dino's chin, first eight inches away and now four. Every second brought it that much closer. Dino resisted with every ounce of muscle he possessed, tried to wriggle away. But the merc was relentless.

Karin saw that her friend was fighting a losing battle. He had seconds left. She rose, then ducked as the hunter fired at her, taking one more chunk of flesh from a dead corpse. She was pinned down.

It was then that Mai regained her feet and chose to strike the remaining trophy hunters. Three of them couldn't withstand her. First an elbow and then a knee, a whirling kick that shattered a cheekbone. A jab of stiffened fingers and a man was bleeding from an eye. She pirouetted among them in a lethal ballet, twisting and turning their bodies and keeping them between her and Valance at the back of the cave, breaking bones and tearing flesh with every passing second. Their guns smashed to the floor; their knives clattered away; their limbs sagged. Suddenly, the fight and the will to chase was out of them.

And then there were no more trophy hunters.

"You went the way all poachers should go," she whispered, on her knees. "Utterly destroyed by their prey."

But her actions caused problems. There was now nothing between her and Valance and the two mercs. Karin was able to attack the merc bearing down on Dino. Punching at the side of his neck. When that didn't work she reached underneath his body and leant her weight to that of Dino's, wrenching the gun so that it moved away from her friend's face and pointed straight at their enemy's.

She pulled the trigger.

Both she and Dino turned away as the man's head exploded. After a moment she rolled the dead body away and dragged Dino back to the two piled up bodies.

"Saved you," she whispered.

"Had . . . had it under control," he stammered back, but she could see by the whiteness of his face and his shaking hands that he had used up almost every ounce of strength in his battle.

Luther was destroying another merc. As Mai took stock she saw that only Valance and his two mercenaries remained. The trouble was they were at the back of the cavern. Their guns were aimed.

"Down!" she cried.

She fell among the bodies. She felt old flesh beneath her; she felt exposed bone. Flies buzzed everywhere. Bullets slammed to left and right. She rolled further away, crunching over several old skeletons. She was in the boneyard proper, the place where the old dead lay. As she scrabbled around, eyeless skulls met her gaze, a ribcage exploded with a series of popping sounds, a leg socket jabbed her in the ribs. An index finger scraped her cheek, drawing blood. She rolled until she came up against something solid.

She looked up.

A cloud of bone dust filled the air. She was next to the rock face. It towered over her like an unattainable dream, full of promise but too deadly to risk. She chanced a look back over her shoulder.

Valance was waving a Glock. His two mercenary friends were sighting along their barrels, trying to pick off Luther. They were advancing. Of course, they had nothing to fear at distance although they remained wary. Frantically, Mai checked around the floor for weapons but came up with nothing except a sharpened tibia. She hoped the other three had been cleverer than her.

Valance advanced. Mai stole through the boneyard she'd just decimated, creeping like a ghost toward dead mercenaries. Karin and Dino stayed low behind two bodies. Luther was barely covered behind two more. Even as she watched, Mai saw a bullet strike through a dead man's arm which had been bitten through by something unknown. The bullet nicked Luther's thigh.

She was almost past the bone dust.

Valance stopped. "You did well, rabbits," he said. "Better than all the rest. The best performance yet. Showy, but solid. But all that ends right now."

Mai wasn't going to be fast enough.

Valance signaled his men. Together the three charged, firing carefully. Bullets slammed into barricades made of meat and bone; the sound was tremendous.

Mai risked it all and broke cover, running for mercs she'd killed earlier that had dropped their guns. She dived headlong as the trail of bullets almost reached Luther.

But it was Dino that rose up. It was Dino that got to his feet amid the hail of bullets and pointed two handguns of his own, one held in each hand. He fired fast and straight from the hip, like a sharpshooter, shot after shot. A bullet skimmed his temple, but he never flinched. Then, a bullet struck him in the chest, sent him staggering back, but Dino never stopped firing, his aim always true. A second bullet hit him, making him cry out, fall to his knees. His fingers never left their triggers.

Karin cried out and flung herself at him, bearing him to the ground. Mai was watching their enemy though. She saw what Dino did to them.

His hail of bullets passed to their left and right, making them flinch before hitting them. First a shot to a man's chest and then, half a second later, another to the same man's stomach. He was already falling when a third bullet smashed through his forehead. The other merc fared no better, taking bullets to the face as he tried to whirl away.

Valance was the one that tagged Dino though, standing tall as his colleagues died, and zeroing in on the Italian. It was Valance that shot Dino twice.

In the process of saving himself though, he forgot one vital thing.

Luther.

Mai saw the huge American propel his body slowly, legs first, around his barricade and toward the next. This one he prized apart, sliding one body off the next, and then crept over like a ghoul slinking among the dead. By the time Valance shot Dino for the second time, Luther was within striking distance.

Valance saw the figure rise from the corner of his eye.

"Shit—"

Luther launched the full weight of his body at the mercenary leader, shattering ribs as he smashed into the man's chest. The gun went flying, clattering off a rock face. Valance folded. Luther caught him as he fell, clamping one huge hand around the man's neck and lifting him off the floor.

"You don't get to die that easy."

Valance kicked but Luther lifted him higher until his heels kicked in space. Valance produced a knife, but Luther still had a spare hand and simply grabbed the wrist and twisted until it snapped. The knife fell away. Luther lifted Valance to the extent of his reach and slammed him back against the rock wall.

"You called our flight a performance," Luther grated. "While we ran for our lives you joked and laughed, chasing us with automatic weapons. I really hope our performance blew you away."

Mai winced as Luther produced the grenade he'd taken earlier, shoved it down the front of Valance's tight bulletproof jacket, pulled the pin, then threw the man back down the tunnel he'd emerged from.

When the explosion came, Mai turned to Karin. "Is he okay?"

"Yeah, thank God they let us keep the flak jackets."

Dino gasped and coughed, clutching the two areas on his chest where the bullets had struck. His face was white.

"Scary," Karin was saying. "That was so scary."

"We're not out of this yet," Mai said. "Now, let's climb!"

CHAPTER TWENTY FOUR

Dahl checked his watch. It was a little after 4 p.m. From their vantage point they could see the Scavenger camp and all the activity down there. They had been forced to abandon their earlier attack when the entire Scavenger force surrounded their friends and sat down, guns resting across their laps, knives at their sides.

"What?" Kenzie had said. "Is it story time?"

A white-bearded, ropy-muscled individual walked before the Scavengers, brandishing a machete.

Kenzie had pulled Dahl to the ground. "We can't attack now unless it's end of days stuff. They're all in the same place and just a few feet from the captives."

Dahl saw it and knew she was right. They hit the dirt and broke out field glasses, shuffled as far forward as they could get. They could hear nothing. Dahl's lip-reading skills explained a little, and the rest could be read between the lines.

Hayden, Kinimaka and Molokai were about to become a part of a ritual. Some ceremony the Scavengers held dear. By all accounts, it was going to be a long one.

Dahl watched as the dead body was removed from the fourth stake. "I still don't understand why they aren't packing."

"They don't care," Dallas said. "And they have nowhere to go."

"We're gonna have to hurry this along," Dahl said. "The nuke clock is ticking."

"Just wait a bit," Kenzie insisted. "Let them get engrossed in their little ceremony. If it's anything like some I've witnessed in the past, it'll take all their attention."

Dahl turned his head. "Oh yeah, like what?"

"I'll explain another time but suffice to say they usually involve inebriates, drugs, smoke, blood and a dozen other things you don't wanna know about."

Dahl studied the camp through the glasses. "I don't like the look of this."

The white-bearded man was opening a gash in his arm, just below the left bicep. Whilst he worked he capered before his captives, whooping and nodding along to an invisible beat. Parts of the audience began to shake their heads too, keeping time to their leader's crazy antics. As blood started to flow he turned to the other arm and parted the flesh there.

To the left, Dahl saw two men behead the corpse they'd dragged off the fourth stake, before shoving it onto a pole. Then they stuck the pole in the ground near the outskirts of their camp. Dallas related the events, keeping his eye on all proceedings.

Dahl's attention was riveted on the center. The white-bearded man was letting his blood drip into a small stone bowl. Others came up, adding their blood to the mix. Hayden, Kinimaka and Molokai watched, fiddling with their bonds, stretching and pulling at the knots. Their hands were bound behind their backs, which would prove useful in hiding their actions, but their ankles were crossed and tied, which was a hindrance. Kinimaka stared wild-eyed at the ceremony unfolding before him, sometimes more engrossed in the ritual than he was with trying to escape.

Dahl kept watching until Kenzie pointed out a smaller

but closer slope from which they could view. They crawled down their own hill and up the next, now just a hundred yards from the Scavenger camp.

Whitebeard held his hands in the air, coming to an abrupt stop. Dahl watched the blood stream down his arms to his shoulders. He lifted the blood-filled bowl. From a pocket he produced a rudimentary brush—a thick twig tied with animal bristles. Next, he stepped up to Molokai and unfastened his bulletproof jacket, letting it flap open. Then he pulled apart the top of his shirt. He dipped the brush in the blood and turned to the audience.

"It begins!" Dahl heard him cry out.

The leader of the Scavengers went to work, painting odd shapes first at the base of Molokai's neck and then on his cheeks and forehead. He used the blood sparingly so that it didn't drip. Once he was satisfied with the outcome, he moved on to Kinimaka and Hayden.

By now, the entire Scavenger group were up on their knees, chanting, nodding their heads in time to the unheard beat. They were glaring at either their captives or their leader, engrossed. Nothing else moved. Nothing else made sound.

The ceremony was everything.

"Now," Kenzie said. "We go now."

CHAPTER TWENTY FIVE

Drake scanned the skyline as they reached the base of the mountain. It wasn't late, but the sun was already tending toward the west. Shadows were lengthening. Good sense dictated they shouldn't be on the top of this mountain at night, yet they had no choice. Hopefully, Mai and the others would be up there.

Sat waiting?

Not likely, but he could dream. And, while he was at it, maybe one of the guys up top could be holding a freshly made bacon sandwich, the kind he liked with crozzled crusts and just a flick of brown sauce. That thought reminded him of Ben Blake—they'd often discussed the merits of rewarding the end of a mission with the good taste of a local Yorkshire bakery—sandwich or otherwise.

Sadness washed through him. It had been a long time since he visited God's Own Country. It had been much longer since he spoke to Ben Blake. There were times, when all was quiet, that he would hear Ben's voice—exactly as it had been—advising or persuading him, pointing out the pros and cons of a situation. Every time it made him pause, made him think. Was it the same for everyone? When you grew so close to a person and then lost them, did they revisit your thoughts when a situation or a memory or just an everyday noise related to something they'd once done or said?

The bacon sandwich scenario filled his mind. Young Blakey would have speculated on the sausage roll alternative, and the dos and don'ts of using ketchup instead of brown sauce. Drake heard it all clearly in his mind as if his old friend was standing at his side. The island vanished. Even Alicia went to the back of his mind, which was never an easy accomplishment.

The world is worse for losing you, old friend. People are dead or lost now because you weren't around to help or save them. My life has followed a different, poorer path without you in it. Maybe, if we meet again, I'll get to tell you all about it.

Wouldn't that be great? Drake thought wistfully. To meet up with the ones you'd loved and lost at some time in the future. To sit, to chat, to love them again, to hug and hold them as long as you liked. To tell them how much you missed them. To talk like you used to. To remember the great, golden glory days when you were all alive.

Drake leaned against a rock, overcome with emotion. The recent deaths of Lauren and Smyth, and the past deaths of those he loved weighed heavy on him now.

Alicia crouched at his side. "You all right, Drakey?"

Somehow, she knew not to interfere too much. "Yeah, yeah. Just processing."

"Take your time."

He figured there would be time enough to process later. And, after everything that had happened during the last week and through recent years, realized it was catching up to him. But he needed time to deal with it.

"You think . . . Hayden's proposal will give us all . . . some space?" he asked.

Alicia gazed into his eyes. "I think it might."

"I wonder how."

"I'm interested to find out."

Drake shrugged it off, straightening his shoulders and

taking a deep breath. Whatever traumas fought inside his head would have to wait. The safety of Mai and the others came first, and then they needed to get the hell off this bloody island.

"After you," Drake said.

Alicia moved out. They were up against the rock face in two minutes. Above rose a jagged black mountain. It would take some careful, skilful climbing to scale it, but there were no other options. They couldn't surreptitiously breach the castle at this point; they didn't have time. Behind, Drake saw the distant forest where the Creepers had been packing up and knew the valleys were beyond that. Hopefully, Dahl and his crew were already rescuing Hayden and the others. Vaguely, he could see the cliffs where they had first set foot on this island over twelve hours ago.

"C'mon." Alicia started up.

Drake stowed his gun, tightened his backpack, and followed her. Soon, they were a third of the way up and resting in a tiny lee.

Alicia stared out, across the land. "I feel like a hobbit," she said. "Heading to Mordor."

"You look like one," Drake attempted to lighten his spirit. "Haven't shaved for a week."

"Yeah, armpits are feeling a little bushy and I'll be needing shears to start the proper topiary down below."

Drake chuckled despite himself. "I meant your beard."

"I know, but if I acknowledged your meaning I'd have to hurt you, and you're looking a bit fragile right now, Drakey."

It was clearly easy to see. "Can't hide my feelings, I guess. Not from you. It's been a long few years, Alicia. So long."

Her eyes sought the horizon, a hundred feet high and

exposed on the small ledge. "We've come back from the brink a hundred times. Saved the world. Found new friends we can trust. Even saved ourselves . . ." She let the sentence hang.

Drake thought about how much she'd changed. "I love that about you," he said. "That you wanted to change and made it happen."

"Not without you though," she said. "Never without you."

They turned their attention back to the mountain, climbing another hundred feet before stopping again. Drake's fingers and feet were aching. His arm, where the flak jacket and undershirt didn't cover it, was grazed. They checked the time—after 5 p.m. Just seven and a half hours to the explosion.

It sounded like they had more than enough time, but there were several factors they couldn't guesstimate. Where was Mai? Where were Dahl and the others? Could they sneak down into the castle? Could they even find a ship?

Seven and a half hours would never be long enough, but it was all they had.

They continued the climb, finally nearing the top. It was then that the one factor they'd forgotten made itself known. The factor they'd long been dreading.

From above, from up on the mountain's summit, there came a loud, terrible, bloodcurdling howl.

CHAPTER TWENTY SIX

Dahl checked the time. It was now or never if they were going to rescue Hayden and the others.

"I don't like the odds," Dallas grumbled.

"The SPEAR team doesn't discuss odds," Dahl said. "We just knock them down."

"Literally," Kenzie said.

"Sixteen of them." Dallas shook his head. "It's suicide."

"Get close," Dahl growled. "No mercy. No fucking about. Free our friends, even if it's just their hands, and give them a gun. Now, man up, because, ready or not, we're about to kick some freakish ass."

Together, they rose and started running, staying low to the ground and as quiet as possible. Their rifles were aimed at their enemies, fingers on triggers. Whitebeard was facing his captives, as were all his men. It was the captives that caught sight of Dahl's attack, but they made no outward sign of it.

Down the slope they ran, hitting level ground only twenty feet from the Scavenger camp. Ahead were potholes, divots, holes in the ground where these men slept, and an assortment of ragged tents. Their approach put the poles where their friends were tied at an angle, so there would be no chance of hitting them with any crossfire.

Dahl slowed just ten feet from the camp. It felt wrong, opening fire indiscriminately, but he knew what would happen if he didn't. The Scavengers would show no mercy in killing them all.

He squeezed his trigger. To left and right Kenzie and Dallas did the same. Bullets stitched a path across the backs of the nearest men, red blooms flourishing. Their dead bodies sagged and fell sideways. Dahl killed two before anyone started moving. Whitebeard was the first to spin and shout a warning. By then, Dallas had killed one man, Kenzie another. Their enemies were rising, not shocked; just looking to defend themselves. Whitebeard stayed right in front of Hayden and bellowed for weapons.

Dahl burst through them, bowling men over. He fired into stomachs and at chests, missing some, winging some, destroying some. Bodies were everywhere. Flashes of fists, legs and machetes filled his vision. He saw a hammer spinning end over end, aimed for his head, but managed to dodge at the last second.

A man stood up directly in front of him. Dahl struck hard but was knocked to the right. A machete flashed. He rolled, off balance, as he hit another Scavenger. Dallas was on his knees, gun kicked from his hands. Kenzie was at his side, battling with another man as she tried to help.

Dahl was ten feet from Molokai.

Again, the machete sliced at his skull. Dahl stepped under it, letting it go over his head, and came face to face with its wielder. A headbutt smashed the man's nose, a knee pulverized his groin and then a rising uppercut broke bones in his jaw. Within seconds, he slithered to the floor.

Dahl spun again, leapt forward. Whitebeard was suddenly right before him. The leader was tall, muscly and covered in the blood that he'd painted on himself. He came at Dahl with a serrated knife.

Dahl didn't confront him head on, but skipped around his right side, turning fast, and was suddenly alongside Molokai.

"Hands free?"

"Not yet."

Crap. He'd been expecting the giant to have freed his hands by now. Dahl turned his attention back to the fight. Whitebeard approached warily, backed by two Scavengers wielding blades. Two more were running to a nearby tent, which was probably where they stored their guns. Dallas was knocking an opponent to the ground. Kenzie had pulled away from her own and was turning her gun on him.

She fired.

He fell, squirming, soon to be dead.

Dahl fired from the hip. A Scavenger fell away, screaming, not dead. A blood-encrusted blade swung at the Swede's face and then jabbed at his chest. Whitebeard came at him without pause, giving him no time for another shot. He twisted to the right, coming alongside Kinimaka. He caught Whitebeard's attack and flung the man away. The knife-wielder was next. Dahl batted the blade to the side with his gun, using the barrel to deflect it. It was a numb move, with no skill, but it was effective.

Still, he was glad Kenzie was too preoccupied to see it.

The knife came back. Dahl had space enough to fire off a shot, but the rifle was too high. Its bullet skimmed the top of the man's head. But it did make him pause, eyes wide with fear as the thought occurred that he'd been shot.

Dahl finished him off with a well-placed bullet to the center of the forehead. The man he'd previously wounded stood, trying to ignore his bleeding side. Whitebeard was on one knee. Dahl cast around.

It was getting desperate. None of their captive friends had managed to loosen their bonds. The Scavengers who'd broke from the tent were emerging, carrying dozens of weapons, almost overbalanced with them, rifle barrels sticking up from their arms like the spines of a gigantic porcupine.

Dahl guessed they had about thirty seconds.

"Fuck!" Last chance.

It was worth the risk. He leapt away from Whitebeard and his other opponent, slipped behind the stakes, pulled out a knife and hacked at Hayden's ropes. It took several seconds to sever the bonds. Her wrists bled profusely. Dahl tugged the last bit of rope away and then put his handgun into the palm of her hand.

He jumped three feet to the left, to Kinimaka.

Hayden brought her gun to the front and covered him, firing three bullets at three targets. Whitebeard managed to dive away. Two Scavengers were hit, falling but alive. Dahl chopped through the big Hawaiian's bonds before giving him his last spare gun. Thank God they had come fully tooled. Dahl then ran to Molokai.

He looked up as he sawed at the ropes. Hayden was fighting hand to hand, still tied by the ankles, trading punches with a Scavenger, unable to escape the stake and bring her gun to bear. Kinimaka had loosed two bullets, killed one man and wounded one for a second time. Two Scavengers charged him wildly, throwing knives to distract his aim. Both weapons struck him with the base of their handles, but it was nonetheless painful. Kinimaka began to heave at the pole that secured him.

It was a crazy scene. Dahl freed Molokai, gave him a knife, which the giant then used to slash the face of the closest man. Hayden traded blows non-stop, boxing style but tied at the ankles, in a highly unusual manner. Whitebeard was screaming at everyone. The men with the guns were throwing them to their colleagues as Kenzie and Dallas rampaged among them.

Kinimaka employed huge strength to heave his stake out of the ground. It came free with a sucking sound, coated with soil. As his attackers neared he managed to swivel fast and hard. The stake, still attached to his back, smashed them both across the face, sending them flying back into the dirt, dazed and hurt. Kinimaka bellowed in anger.

Dahl emerged from behind Molokai. There were nine Scavengers left, three of whom were wounded. Dallas fought one, Kenzie another. It wasn't going to be enough. The plan had counted on their friends getting free swiftly and it hadn't happened.

Three Scavengers held guns and were training them first on Kenzie and then on Hayden and Molokai. They were easy targets and would be the first to die.

Dahl moved to stand in front of Hayden.

"Not while I still live," he said.

The whole Scavenger camp shimmered with white-hot violence. No quarter asked or given. It was kill or be killed, and the SPEAR team did their best to fight as one. Dallas knocked Kenzie to the ground a second before she would have been shot through the head. A bullet whizzed over his spine. Dallas rolled on the ground and fired a shot between his ankles. It flew off, missing its target, but sending the man into a tumble nevertheless. Dahl braced himself for another attack, but it never came. Suddenly, he realized he couldn't stop the next shots that would end their lives.

He fired his own bullet, but more Scavengers had fallen back to take up weapons and were focusing on the SPEAR team. Whitebeard was bellowing for their deaths. Every living Scavenger now had a gun and was being quick and efficient about lining figures up in his sights. It all happened so fast Dahl saw there was no chance of escape.

"Torsten," he heard Hayden's voice at his back. "It's an

honor to die with you, my friend."

Then she spoke to Kinimaka, "I think I love you, Mano."

Dahl saw the Scavengers arranging themselves like a firing squad, lining all six of them up. They were arrayed far and wide, impossible to target one man without getting shot by another. Dahl knew he was just one of six, but every death would ring deeply in his heart and soul. *What a terrible time to die. I never thought I'd go out this way.*

Nobody flinched as the shots rang out.

CHAPTER TWENTY SEVEN

Dahl blinked in surprise. He'd been staring straight at the man that fired the shot, expecting to be killed instantly. Already, final thoughts were flitting like errant shadows through his mind. As expected his last vision was of his children but before that, surprisingly, it was Kenzie.

But she was here, after all. He pacified himself with that.

The oddest thing was—when the Scavenger fired, his own head exploded.

Dahl struggled to take it in. Scavengers were falling and throwing themselves to the ground all over their camp. A split second later he understood why.

The other clans were attacking. On foot, and riding trucks, they attacked the Scavenger camp with what looked like vengeful fury. Dahl would have cheered their appearance but knew how close to death he still was. There would be no quarter offered by the other three clans. Dahl and the others dropped to the earth as their entire surroundings erupted into chaos.

It was a well-organized attack. The Marauders—who Dahl recognized from their clothing—ran in from the west, seven men flowing down a steep slope, guns blazing. Two more clans—the Creepers—carried bows—and the Hunters, came in from the east. The Creepers ran fast, twenty strong, spreading out along a ridge alongside a modified truck. The Hunters clung to the framework of their rusted truck, bouncing through divots, trying to aim weapons and hang on at the same time.

Bullets flew everywhere and without perfect aim. Hot metal ripped through the air inches above the prone SPEAR team. Dahl clung to his rifle and swiveled his body so that he could look over at them.

"Don't know what the hell happened but I'm glad it did," he yelled.

"It's payback," Kenzie said. "I recognize a few of the attacker's clothes from the men we saw being tortured and killed at the stake. I'm guessing the other clans decided to wreak a little vengeance on the worst clan on the island before escaping."

"It's a blitz." Molokai shuffled in close. "Full firepower to wipe them out in quick time. Look out!"

From the right came the Creepers' truck, wheels pounding over the ground. Dahl half rose and threw himself out of its way, reeling away from the rushing wind of its passing. The engine noise filled his head for two seconds before it was gone.

Scavengers rose and fired and fought. Knives clashed. Machetes were flung, end over end, their gleaming blades catching the early evening light. Dahl saw a military blade thrown, dripping blood, to wedge into the spine of a Creeper. In return, two Creepers flung themselves onto the Scavenger and pounded down on his body, arrows clutched in their hands. Their victim's screams lasted whole minutes and were horrible.

Men shouted; the truck roared around the camp, catching men with its spiked wheel arches, flinging them through the air. Dahl was amazed at the contrasting clans and the weapons they used: from a spear launched high into the air by a Creeper to the RPG resting over a Marauder's shoulder.

Whitebeard was on his feet, fighting hard. The man

appeared to feel no pain, taking blows to the stomach, face and ribs without slowing or even wincing. His bloody axe swept left and right, keeping men at bay and slicing those that came in too close. Blood coated the grass at his feet. A spear grazed the top of his right shoulder, ripping flesh as it flew past, but he gave it no heed.

Molokai pointed through over the valley's numerous slopes. "The river again," he said. "We can use the rafts to get away."

Hayden who, until now, seemed to be basking on the fact that they had all endured the unendurable, nodded and checked her weapon. "With me."

She scrambled off through the grass. The fighting was becoming more localized, moving toward the center of the Scavenger camp. The rusted truck rumbled to a halt, disgorging its passengers. The Hunters fell upon the remaining Scavengers without mercy.

Dahl crawled in Molokai's wake, staying as low as possible. The grass was only knee high, but the Scavengers were the center of attention for the attackers.

They reached the outskirts of the camp and came in sight of the rushing river. Hayden broke cover and ran to the banks. Kinimaka was a step behind. Dahl took a moment to sit up and stared back at the camp.

The fight was petering out. Whitebeard was on his knees, slashed and bloody. The clans were deliberately making his death the hardest. Only two other Scavengers remained, and they were being herded by men with automatic weapons.

Both Scavengers chose to attack at once, reduced to using knives and a thick, nail-studded branch, but met a hail of gunfire. Their bodies were riddled and danced for several seconds before falling to the floor. Now, Dahl finally stood up and walked away. He saw the truck brought up. Four men strapped Whitebeard to its front grill, a horrendous hood ornament covered in blood, head lolling, tongue sticking out of his mouth.

Men piled into the truck and arranged themselves around it. Nobody thought to check around for the SPEAR team.

These men, it seemed, had another pressing purpose.

Before jumping into the dinghy, Dahl wondered where the clans might be going next, because it sure didn't look like they were ready to leave the island. Were they embarking on another revenge mission? If so, against whom?

Finally, he held on tight as the Zodiac bearing all six of them began to flow and skim through the river, bound for the mountain where Drake and Alicia were, hopefully, close to saving Mai.

CHAPTER TWENTY EIGHT

Drake reached the top of the cliff first, rolling over the edge and onto the mountain's summit. His initial impression was that it was empty; his second that the view was fantastic.

Hair grazed by the wind, face warmed by the dying sun, he gazed in all four directions as Alicia pulled herself up. Every horizon was dominated by the blue ocean, deep and seemingly endless. A mirror image of it hung in the skies, broken only infrequently by tatters of white cloud.

The tops of trees marked the forest to the south, the darkness within the close-growing boughs a fitting shadow on the island. Beyond them he saw the valley slopes still brushed by sunlight, greens and browns standing out in patchwork patterns. To the far south he saw the area they hadn't visited, the wilderness, where the Hunters lived, a barren, brown land that appeared to consist of deep holes, carved into the ground. Old mines, perhaps. A dust haze rose off the land there.

Closer now, he studied the top of the mountain. It was a sloping, dark-colored rock surface, slanted to the eastern rim that overlooked the castle and docks. That side was where a jagged group of rocks protruded higher and Drake could see three cave entrances among them. The north was where shrubs and stunted trees grew, running away from the mountain and down its oceanward slope, all the way to the crashing, foaming waters. The west was barren—just pure rock running all the way to the edge.

"Not many options," Alicia said, staring between the

caves and the tree cover. "And no sign of the Sprite."

"She'll be here." Drake hoped he didn't sound too desperate. They had no idea what dangers Mai had encountered inside the mountain.

"No sign of any . . . monsters," Alicia whispered, rolling her shoulders to ease tension from the climb.

"Don't say that," Drake said. "You'll jinx it."

"Soldiers don't work that way," Alicia said.

"We're not in the Army anymore. Let's check the trees."

He stopped when the howling began. He glanced over at Alicia.

"It's not me," she said.

Drake gulped. It wasn't an animal howling, not a wolf or a coyote. It came from a tortured throat. From a being hurt beyond repair and recognition.

It was a human sound.

Drake trained his gun on the trees. Alicia tightened a finger on her trigger. "If anything moves in there, I'm shooting first and asking questions later."

"Just be careful it isn't a pack of friendly raccoons."

"Does it sound like a fucking raccoon?"

"Dunno, love. I never heard a raccoon howl before."

The trees rustled and swayed and then four figures broke clear. Drake hesitated, grimacing, unsure exactly what was coming at them. Then, he realized. It was men; broad, large men who, at one time, were probably mercenaries. Somehow, their bodies had become disfigured. From misshapen faces to irregular skulls; from arms that appeared to have been broken and badly reset to warped and crooked fingers. They loped out of the treeline, still screaming, howling in pain and bloodlust, and came straight for Drake and Alicia.

"What do we do?" the Englishwoman asked.

"I don't want to shoot, but hell, if we don't defend ourselves we're gonna die."

In counterpoint to his words, more howls erupted from the forest. Drake swallowed drily. "How many of them are there?"

"And how do they live up here?"

"I think the Devil has been helping everyone on the quiet," Drake said, still preparing. "All the clans, I mean. Guns. Ammo. Provisions. Maybe medicines. It's why he's so broke."

"All this talk of the Devil," Alicia said. "All this knowledge. And we still don't know what he looks like."

Drake saw the issues with that. "Yeah, but that's a future problem."

Out of options and with the cliff at their back, Drake and Alicia opened fire. Their bullets took down all four attackers, sending them writhing to the ground. Drake ran forward and ended their lives quickly, wincing as he saw the faces up close.

"What the hell did this to them?"

"Experiments." Alicia shuddered. "I hate to imagine."

The chorus of howls grew louder, resounding among the trees like a ghoulish choir. The eastern skies were darkening too as the sun set to the west, throwing long shadows over the top of the mountain. Drake couldn't see between the boughs. Slowly, Alicia and he walked forward, keeping an eye to the caves on their right. More screaming erupted ahead and then the trees began to shake as if a great hand had grabbed them. The screams were so agonized Drake couldn't imagine they came from a human throat.

In reality, they didn't, he thought. These genetic experiments were far from human now.

They broke through the treeline, a dozen sparsely clothed, disproportionate, barely human figures, brandishing thick branches and carrying large rocks, bellowing with fury as they attacked. Drake raised his gun but a dozen rocks filled the air, aimed at him and Alicia. He flinched away, unable to evade them all, firing as accurately as he could. One attacker collapsed before Drake was struck by a rock. It bounced off his right arm, upsetting his aim, and then another crashed into his jacket just below his throat.

He staggered back. Alicia shot two runners before taking a blow to the top of the head which sent her to her knees.

Nine more came on fast, closing the gap.

Drake re-sighted, fired at an awkward angle, and took out another. Alicia fumbled her weapon up and let loose a volley, smashing two more across the legs. More rocks struck Drake hard, glancing off his armor. One caught him just above the right eye, drawing blood and making him fold. Their enemy leapt at them.

Drake rolled as a man landed on his right side, shrugged him off. He came up on his knees, brought the rifle around, but then another body slammed into his back, sending him sprawling next to his first opponent. He rolled. A rock came down at his face. Drake brought an arm up, blocking it, but felt sharp pain from his elbow to his wrist as the rock struck.

Alicia had kicked out as their attackers closed in. She swept the legs of one man and heard his face smash into the rock as another jumped at her. She managed to guard against the kick, using his momentum to throw him beyond her. She swiveled again, gaining space. She looked up.

Four men leapt on top of her.

Drake fought his two attackers. Two wounded men

dragged themselves toward him as if desperate to be part of the fight. One of the bigger issues was making sure his opponents didn't get hold of a weapon. He heaved one man away, then turned to another and whipped out his knife.

He sliced the man's throat and spun back.

The second man rushed in hard, straight onto the blade. Drake held it steady for a few seconds before wrenching it free. The man collapsed.

He checked on Alicia.

Shit!

The blonde was being dragged away. Two men had firm hold of her ankles whilst two more pulled her arms. Almost spread-eagled, she was being hauled across the top of the mountain toward the trees.

Alicia shouted and struggled. Drake was surprised to see her words having no effect since they were top-drawer Myles critical masterpieces. He stalked forward, raising his rifle. Of the two wounded men still dragging themselves across the floor, one half-rose and launched a huge boulder. Drake ducked, turned and killed him. Then he lined up on the first of the four men dragging Alicia.

A shot and he fell dead, freeing one of her legs. They were close to the treeline now, just crossing the underbrush. Drake had to hurry.

His next shot fell on an empty chamber.

Bollocks. He'd been so preoccupied with the fight that he'd forgotten to keep count. Another glaringly obvious telltale sign that he wasn't a soldier anymore. Alicia kicked and squirmed, unbalancing her captors, who pulled up for a moment.

A rock smashed against Drake's back. He slammed home a new mag, turned and took care of the other wounded man. Then whirled back to the front.

"Stop playing with yourself and get these fuckers off me, Drake," Alicia shouted.

Drake waited a moment more. Both men holding Alicia's arms let go and picked up large rocks. It looked like they were about to dash the heavy boulders into her face. Drake shot one through the head.

Movement from the right caught his attention and made him whip his head toward the cave entrances, trepidation flooding his system with ice water.

He saw Mai Kitano running out into the open, shielding her eyes at first, but then spotting Drake and sprinting toward him.

"Mai!" he shouted.

"Drake!" she cried back.

"For fuck's sake!" Alicia bellowed and covered up as an attacker smashed a rock down at her face. It impacted with her right bicep, making her grunt, but she grabbed the wrist of her attacker and threw him to the ground.

That left the two men that were holding her ankles apart.

Mai pulled up short, shaking her head. "What the hell is Taz up to now? That's a new low, Alicia, even for you."

Drake smiled as he finished off both men, allowing Alicia the chance to sit up and brush off. By that time Luther, Karin and Dino were running up to them.

"Any pursuit?" Drake asked.

"No, we killed them all."

"Perfect."

Alicia stalked up, giving everyone a death glare. "About time you lot showed up. How was the cave tour?"

Mai just shook her head. Drake looked to the sunset that had started to spread west. It would soon be dark. "Right," he said. "The bomb's still ticking away but we do have time to defuse it. And we need to rescue the prisoners in that compound. Mai—we'll explain." He checked the time. "About six hours to detonation. I think we should rest here for a short while and give Dahl a chance to catch up."

He sat down on the edge of the cliff, legs dangling, facing the western horizon and its splendid yellow and burnished orange sunset, and the others sat next to him.

CHAPTER TWENTY NINE

Staying with the river, Hayden found that it ultimately twisted toward the castle but, for a while at least, brought them closer to the mountain that overlooked it. The river was a quick series of sharp and sweeping bends, lefts and rights, punctuated by small rapids. Among them, only Dahl appeared to be enjoying the ride but then that was to be expected.

She took the silent moments of the journey to reflect. Back at the Scavenger camp, all in the space of thirty minutes, she'd thought she was going to die twice. First at the stake and then before the impromptu firing squad. The only compensation had been that Mano was at her side.

Time to move forward, she thought.

The river dipped suddenly, making her tighten her fingers to cling to the side of the dinghy. Foamy waters lashed her face. She glanced at her colleagues. As soon as they got clear of this island she was going to propose a new strategy, a blueprint that would let them enjoy a future as well as help save the world. Given recent circumstances she was almost certain President Coburn would back it.

It would mean creating a brand new special ops directive, but countries did that all the time.

She felt quiet excitement. She couldn't wait to tell them. Somehow, they'd get Yorgi involved too. She hoped the young Russian was safe in Russia, recovering from his wounds. The new Blood King was still out there, after all.

The river turned and fell about three feet. Hayden hung

on. Her clothing was soaked. Her body ached, cut and bruised from this day's fighting. In truth, she'd become used to it. But the body and the mind could only take so much.

Kinimaka was a good cushion to her left. She allowed herself to press into him whenever the situation allowed. He didn't seem to mind. There was a distant smile on the big man's face. Maybe the river journey was bringing back old Hawaiian memories. Hayden hoped so.

Around the Zodiac, Kenzie and Dallas conversed as best they could. Dahl was invested in the ride. Molokai sat hunched over, having pulled his jacket and his single robe about him. Maybe it was his way of cutting himself off from the world, of decompressing. Maybe he was in pain. They still didn't know much about Luther's big brother.

Except that he was fiercely loyal, and effective in a fight. Whatever baggage he brought along was his to keep, or to share. They all had their demons.

She thought about her father, the example of the perfect cop he'd left behind for her to follow. JJ had been gunned down in a convenience store. There were days when she couldn't quite remember the full contours of his face, the aspect of his smile. It pained her now because, back then, it was all she lived for. Making her father smile had been the highlight of her day.

But he had helped mold her into the person she was today. Not once had he coerced her into following his footsteps, into living up to his name. She'd brought all that on herself. Finally though, now, with Mano, and the SPEAR team so well established, she knew that she was content with the person she'd become.

"You see that?" Dahl was knelt at the front of the boat, totally upright like a Springer Spaniel staring out the window of the car. Hayden imagined his tongue was probably hanging out.

"Can't see anything," Dallas groaned. "Feel sick."

"Water doesn't agree with you?" Kenzie pounced. "I thought you were ex-Army."

"Water. Air. Any kind of travel. Being Army doesn't make you less motion-sick."

"Well, that limits your options. How come you never said anything before?"

"I was . . . manning up."

"That just makes it worse. You know, I'll have to dock your pay."

"Funny. You're so funny."

"Hey!" Dahl shouted. "You can moan at each other later. Eyes up front."

Everyone caught the tone of the Swede's voice and shuffled around. Hayden struggled into an upright position, on her knees. The river ran dead straight for a while with grassy, muddy banks and several fallen trees but there was nothing else to obstruct their view.

To the left the mountain rose, and beyond it they could now see the Devil's castle. It was where he lived, the place he'd defended against the clans for the last several years. It was where the compounds and the keep and the docks lay. Where the only means of getting off this doomed island lay. Hayden studied the high walls with their crenellations, the weapons she could see poking out, the guards on the walls, the pockmarks in the wall which were undoubtedly the scene of earlier assaults. She could also see the entrance—a pair of high, straight steel doors, like garage roller shutters. Somehow, they looked wrong at the front of the castle, but she could understand the logic.

Especially now.

Because, coming across the plains, riding vehicles and running and marching on foot came the clans and all their men. They carried every weapon they had, they carried their belongings, they brandished bows and rifles and RPGs and spears. Their truck bristled with all manner of armament—from improvised, spiked cow-catchers to large projectiles. Men crowded the bed and balanced atop the cab. Behind it came at least seventy more warriors.

Dahl motioned at them. "They're trying to finish this," he said. "It's about five hours to the explosion. Maybe they're going after the ships?"

"Or wealth," Molokai grunted. "The Devil's bound to have gold inside. It's an unshakeable commodity."

"That would make sense," Dahl said. "Plus, I doubt they have warm feelings for this Devil character. He's saved and destroyed their lives more than once. On this island, despite all its aberrations, its brutes and beasts, he's the real monster."

Kenzie inspected her weapons. "I guess we have about twenty minutes until they start their battle," she said. "And we have a mountain to climb."

Hayden looked to the left. The mountain and everything it offered reared with implacable disdain. It was eternal, unlike them. She braced herself as Dahl and Kinimaka guided the Zodiac to the nearest level bank. Water collided with the side of the raft. She saw animals that looked like rabbits dashing off into the undergrowth. The loamy smell of rotting vegetation replaced the fresh air she'd experienced amid the rushing water. The Zodiac hit earth with a solid impact, sending her into Molokai. No apology was necessary. She picked herself up and eyed the bank.

"Easy climb." Dahl was gauging the mountain. "Just stick to the rocky bits there." He pointed at a series of outcroppings and ledges that ran all the way to the top. "Anyone encounters trouble—yell."

She jumped onto the bank and felt her boots sink into the mud. She shrugged her pack tighter around her shoulders and started to walk. Soon, they were up against the mountain.

"I hope to God Drake's up there," Dahl said, peering up.

"I'll tell him you said that." Kinimaka grinned.

"Um, no." Dahl grimaced. "I'd really rather you didn't."

"And Mai," Hayden said, then paused. "Hey, was that gunfire?"

As one, they peered back toward the plains, the running clans, the truck and the castle. Hayden saw that they were still some minutes away from engagement.

More shots rang out. Looking up, Hayden knew they were coming from the mountain top.

"Quickly," Dahl said. "Fast as you can. We have to help them!"

CHAPTER THIRTY

The Devil viewed this startling new development with interest from the top floor of his keep.

Not once did I imagine they'd attack.

He'd been planning on leaving, exiting the door of his surveillance room, when word had come in about a large force of men streaming toward the castle. At first, the Devil thought someone was playing tricks. There wasn't a large force of men on the island; all the clans were divided.

But then he'd started to wonder.

He shook his head in bewilderment. All these years . . . all these years they'd fought and killed and ignored each other. They tortured each other. On occasion, three clans had watched whilst the fourth assaulted his castle, dying as they came, and they had laughed. But now . . .

The fickle and unpredictable quirks of men.

He thought about the bomb ticking away below and checked the time. Five hours to go. Perhaps the clans wanted something other than his death. He found it hard to believe—he was the focal figure on the island and such an infamous killer after all—but there were other things here that might attract the clans.

Quickly, he reviewed his plans. The job in Washington DC was already streamlined and unstoppable, just awaiting his arrival. The ships were all but loaded and ready to go. The prisoners had been given their false hope, told they would be set free very soon. His mercenaries were on standby, ready for anything.

The problem was—if they left the castle undefended, the clans would gain entry and perhaps have a chance of sinking some ships. Any ships. Perhaps, if luck went against him, *his* ship.

He identified several RPGs and many large caliber rifles among the crazy mix of weapons approaching the castle walls.

The Devil unhooked his radio from its belt clip and thumbed the mic button. "Defend the castle," he said. "Keep those wolves from our door. All I ask is for their total annihilation."

It was enough for the men in his service. There was plenty of time remaining before detonation and they would all know that. He didn't expect mutiny, but he always prepared for it. The Devil then radioed his own ship and told its captain to be ready to depart at a moment's notice.

A delicious distraction now presented itself.

It had been a long time since the Devil fought a real battle. Even the thought of it stirred the animal inside. He took a quick tour around his own private armory, tooling up not only for a battle but for the long voyage to America he would soon have to endure. He would be relatively vulnerable until they reached the newly named town of Devil's Junction.

For now, though, let's see what damage the Devil can do.

Soon, he was up on the castle walls, looking out through a crenellation, standing alongside two dozen men. The long, wide, flat plain that formed the approach to his gates fairly rumbled with the approaching force. It wasn't the size of the attack, it was the volume and combination of weapons they brought. And the thrill he felt wasn't just for the impending battle—it was knowing that this was the clans' last assault, their final chance to breach the castle and kill the Devil—the instigator of all their woes.

Squinting hard, he saw the big truck approaching sported a dreadful hood ornament. A wounded man. The Devil thought he recognized him as the leader of the Scavengers. He grinned.

A fitting end.

As it approached, the truck accelerated.

So that was their plan. To be fair, the clansmen didn't have many options. The Devil was reasonably confident the castle doors would hold . . . until a man rose in the back of the truck.

"RPG!" someone shouted out.

It wasn't anything they hadn't tried before. But this time the clans were desperate. And this time they were united.

From the midst of the runners, two more men emerged carrying rocket launchers. As one, all three fired their grenades at the castle doors. The Devil and his men ducked, taking cover behind the heavy concrete walls. Explosions rocked the very foundations, making the ledge they stood on shudder and shake. Cracks appeared in the blocks in front of the Devil's eyes. He could imagine that three grenades might buckle the doors. At worst, it would weaken them.

The truck hit the gates too, strengthened cow-catcher and Scavenger leader at the front taking the brunt of the impact.

There came a shrieking, grinding noise like nothing he had ever heard before. The Devil winced, rising just in time to see the rear of the truck bounce back. Windows had shattered, three men had been thrown clear and turned into ragged messes. The small army that followed stalled as it saw their plan hadn't worked.

The Devil grinned, raised his gun and signaled his men. "Kill everyone."

But the truck was still running, still active. The Devil couldn't see what a jumbled mess his castle doors had become, even though they still blocked the entrance. The truck driver could. He backed up a hundred yards, revved the engine and then came again, spinning tires as he gave it everything he could.

Bullets slammed down at the oncoming vehicle, shredding the top of the cab, the sides and what remained of the windshield. The driver jerked spasmodically, hit a dozen times. But the truck came on, smashing into the castle once more.

This time it crashed right through the door and kept going into the courtyard before coming to a stop. The entire remaining force of the island's clans followed it.

The Devil joined his men in opening fire on them. His weapon, a Steyr AUG—as well as being lightweight and robust it offered a change of barrel and the option to attach a KCB-77 bayonet, an idea which the Devil loved—bucked in his hands as he unleashed a storm of lead.

It seemed improper when his enemies fired back.

He stood still for a moment, not quite believing it, but then allowed one of his men to drag him to cover. Below, in the courtyard, more men attacked the stalled truck and the clansmen that came in behind it, using it for cover. Bullets flew. He stared at the scene: the courtyard that encompassed the castle's inner buildings, the open gate to the east that led to the docks, the beach and the ocean beyond.

They needed to hold the clans here.

"Fight!" he shouted. "Fight for everything you want. Either you sail from here today, or you die here today."

In a lull he heard more distant gunfire and turned his eye upward, toward the top of the mountain where the experiments ran free. Who was fighting up there? His experiments were feral, as untamed as nature's most savage concoction. He was proud of them, despite their failures. He'd been trying to replicate the old CIA's mind control program codenamed MKUltra, developing drugs that could be used in torture interrogations to weaken a subject through mind control.

In the '50s and '60s the Scientific Intelligence Division and Special Operations Division were allegedly involved in uncounted illegal operations where they used unwitting US and Canadian test subjects to carry out undisclosed missions, manipulating people's mental states by altering their brain functions, attained by special drugs, hypnosis, sensory deprivation, isolation and various forms of torture.

The Devil had gone a long way to realizing the same ends before lack of money, the escape into the island of the clans, and private work had forced him to quit the program and unleash the monsters he had created. After that, they became legend.

So, who was up on the mountain right now, fighting them? Could it be Mai Kitano and her team? Someone else?

It doesn't matter, the Devil thought, training his Steyr once more on the embattled men. *My monsters will win. I created almost a hundred of them.*

CHAPTER THIRTY ONE

Drake sat with his back to the trees that covered the north side of the mountain top, basking in the sunset. The island's river rushed along below and to the left as they watched the remaining clans attack the castle.

"It's a complication," Alicia said.

"I think it's time to head down," Luther said. "We've been waiting up here for a while now. Just try the comms once more, Drake."

The Yorkshireman was already on it. "Static." He tapped his ear. "The river must have knocked their earpieces out."

Mai leaned back. "I hope you're not thinking of heading down through the cave system, my friends."

Both Karin and Dino made warning sounds.

"Well, you made it out okay," Alicia replied. "Can't be too hard."

Luther shrugged his shoulders. "She had a whole lot of help from a whole lot of man."

"Don't encourage her," Mai muttered. "She'll never stop."

Darkness stole across the land at a steady rate, eating fields and forests and every trace of the horizon to right and left. Gunfire erupted below. It was mostly for this reason that the SPEAR team didn't hear the monsters that crept out of the trees behind them. It was also because they crawled on knees and elbows, staying low to the ground. It was because they were silent, their brains long since having lost the capacity to speak. It was because they snuck along like monstrous spiders, eyes wide and focused on their prey; blood-encrusted bodies as dark as the shadows that clung to them.

Drake heard a noise. It struck him first as odd, because it came from in front, not behind. It came from the space underneath his boots.

"Whoa," he cried out, shocked.

Faces loomed from below, climbing fast. First, he saw Dahl and then Molokai. He grinned widely, but then held his breath, hoping and willing four more figures would follow.

They did. Dahl paused a step below, unable to keep the grin from spreading across his own face. "Taking a break are you, mate?"

"Where have you been?" Drake complained. "You've missed the bloody battle."

"Not down there we haven't." Dahl accepted the proffered arm and pulled himself up. "They're attacking the castle."

"Yeah, which means the ships too." Drake hauled the big Swede over the edge as Molokai accepted Luther's help further down the line. The two brothers were also smiling at each other, just happy to meet again while they were alive.

"We gotta move." Hayden raised her voice so that everyone heard. "Without ships, we're swimming to Guam. Or Japan."

"Don't really swim—" Dallas began, but then stopped speaking in shock as Dahl exploded past Drake.

The Yorkshireman reared back in surprise, but then turned and bellowed out a warning. "Incoming!"

The monsters howled as they crashed into the group at pace. It was all the SPEAR team could do to hold their ground. There was no margin for error since the edge of the cliff was at their backs. Hayden and Kinimaka were still below, clinging to the rock face, unsure whether they should continue to climb or start a descent.

Drake didn't have time to debate an escape plan. These new attackers had clearly been waiting for darkness to fall and were strong in number. He dropped a shoulder, leaned into an assault, then used the momentary confusion to grab his opponent by both shoulders, turn and fling him off the cliff.

"Look out!" Kinimaka cried. "That almost hit me!"

Drake looked down the line, saw Luther and Mai, Dino and Karin standing toe to toe with their aggressors. Closer still were Alicia and Dahl, Kenzie and Molokai—the SPEAR team meeting every onslaught head on with the cliff's edge at their heels.

Wasn't it always this way? Drake thought the strong, poignant image was very telling. He couldn't remember a time when death hadn't either been at their backs or in their faces.

A snarling face filled his vision. A blood-smeared arm struck at his head. Drake caught it, drew his handgun and fired. The body collapsed. He fired again and again. They piled up before him. Still more scrambled over the top. He shot up into their faces. When an attacker jumped down uninjured, Drake smashed him in the face with a Kevlar-covered shoulder, breaking a nose, then used his military knife to end it quickly.

Down the line, his colleagues fought. It wasn't a fair fight. Their assailants could only trust to luck to beat such heavily armed opponents. But there were near misses—hair raising moments. Karin saved Dino from receiving a nasty bite to the back of the hand. Dino didn't sound overly pleased about it. Luther and Molokai built up the biggest body count, using arms and fists as well as weapons. Dahl took time to haul both Hayden and Kinimaka up to safety.

"Just in case the Yorkshire twat decides to throw anyone else at you," he clarified for everyone's sake.

But they were still under pressure. Drake pushed through dead bodies to get a better view. The unfortunate attackers were spread out across the entire area. One launched a spear. It quivered as it flew. Kenzie pushed Dallas aside as it fell toward them, its sharpened point sinking deep into a corpse. Drake saw other spears being launched. Alicia was at his side now. Together they fired on the throwers, taking them down. Mai and Dahl were a step behind, trying to take out spearmen before they threw their weapons. Volleys of bullets crossed the mountain top. The darkness that enveloped them was almost complete, shot through with flourishes of gray.

Five minutes later it was over. The SPEAR team produced flashlights and surveyed the scene.

"We didn't get them all," Hayden said.

"No," Kenzie said. "Some of them still have the good sense to retreat."

"I think the nuke will be a blessing," Kinimaka said, "to them."

"Cleansing fire," Mai agreed.

"Right," Hayden spoke up. "To those rocks. If we climb over the first one to the right we should find an easy way down the mountain, all the way to the beach. It isn't guarded because the Devil thought his monsters were enough."

"Who told you that?" Mai asked as they walked.

"Tolley," Hayden said. "Tolley told me that. A good man. Without his help we might not have survived this island."

They paused at the top of the first rock, looking down on

the floodlit scene below. The courtyard crawled from end to end with men, fighting and screaming. Flashes of gunfire burst forth like random pyrotechnic displays. Men fought on the walls, on the ground and even on the beach. The docks were a melee of combat.

"And we're heading right on down into that?" Dallas asked.

Dahl glanced at him. "It's what we do."

"Yeah, man." Alicia waved a hand. "This is just another day ending in Y for us."

"If we didn't need one of those ships, or to rescue the prisoners, I'd pass," Hayden affirmed. "But there's no choice."

"Don't forget disarming that bomb," Dahl said.

Minutes before, she'd called their own plane to come back and help. It was on its way. But everyone agreed that they couldn't rely on an incoming rescue craft like they could rely on one sitting plainly at anchor below. Especially where a nuke was concerned.

"Time for one last battle on this blasted Devil's island," Hayden said.

Drake followed her down the mountain.

CHAPTER THIRTY TWO

The SPEAR team hurried along as fast as they dared. Drake felt energized by the fact that they were all together again. It didn't matter that they were heading straight into another pitched battle.

They had a plan.

With a horizon marked by the ascending silver moon, and the splendid vista of the rolling ocean with its half dozen ships moored offshore, they approached the base of the mountain. It led them to the very rear of the Devil's courtyard, where there was no fighting, only pitch-black shadow. The main area of combat was at the front and then spread out toward the beach.

Hayden placed her pack on the floor. Many long hours had passed since they'd prepared for this mission. They'd used a bespoke CIA facility to do so, knowing something of what they were up against, and these days a military pack usually came complete with a mini Geiger counter. Hayden found it after just a few seconds of rummaging and switched it on.

"This way."

The device screeched and whirred as she swept it from side to side. If the plutonium core had been exposed, it would leave a signature. The readings ran highest ahead. Hayden set off, flanked by Kinimaka and Molokai, weapons poised and at the ready. Back here, they were shielded by the keep, which stood between them and the battle, but that didn't stop a Marauder from dashing around, spying them and getting shot for his troubles.

Hayden stopped at the rear of the keep. "The reading jumps like crazy here. I gotta say—the bomb's inside."

"And the bloody door's around the front." Alicia sighed. "I have to point out—our luck's deserted us since the Sprite returned."

"Luck is still having your good health and beauty," Mai said. "Or in your case—your health. And my skills to save your ass, of course."

"Oh, save me by finding the door." Alicia made a face as she followed Drake around front.

"It's right in your ass, along with my boot," Kenzie put in, saving Mai the job.

Drake came around cautiously. Here, they were completely exposed. Dahl jumped to the keep's tall wooden door and turned the handle, but to no avail. He took a moment to shoot the lock off. Drake and the others stayed as deep in shadow as possible, still covering the Swede as they assessed the chaos.

Wide steel gates had been smashed and crushed, damaged almost beyond recognition. A truck stood several yards inside, its windows smashed and bloody, its front end and cabin bent out of shape. Bodies lay all around it, most bearing terrible wounds. Men fought hand to hand and ducked behind crates, oil drums, an old van, piles of timber and blocks, and another truck that clearly hadn't moved for months. They traded bullets.

Several clansmen broke from cover and sprinted for the gap that led to the docks and the beach. Two were shot in the back, but four ran through. A merc rose to give chase but was shot dead.

Dahl shoulder-barged the door along with Molokai. Drake experienced deja-vu from their desperate escape attempt back at the Moulin Rouge. Both soldiers fell inside as the door gave way. Alicia followed.

"Stand up boys," she proclaimed. "No need to grovel."

The interior was an antechamber where a winding staircase led upward. A single door lay to the right. Hayden swept the Geiger counter around, stopping at the door.

"In here."

"Wait," Dahl said as they pressed forward. "Wouldn't it make more sense to split up? We do have two missions before we head for the ships."

"He's got a point," Drake said. "So, who here can disarm a bomb?"

"I've disarmed a nuke before," Dahl said. "Back in New York."

"That was with a sledge hammer," Drake said as Dallas' eyes widened. "Anyone else?"

"Me," Molokai said. "I have some history with bombs."

Drake wondered at the wistful, sad face before looking to Kenzie, who was waving. "You too?"

"Yeah, Dallas and I will go with them."

"We will?" Dallas wondered. "I don't like—"

"Yeah, yeah. You don't like flying, sailing, rafting, swimming or playing with bombs. We get it." Kenzie shoved him at Dahl. "Start walking."

Drake waited as Hayden handed Dahl the Geiger counter. It didn't feel right that they should part again so soon. A sudden flurry of bullets struck the building, lending sharper urgency to the dilemmas they had to overcome. He watched as Dahl opened the inner door and stepped through, the others just behind.

He watched as they descended into the pitch-dark, hoping to locate a nuclear bomb.

"I agree it's a crappy situation," Hayden said, turning away back to the outer door. "But it's all we've got and it's the right one."

Drake agreed. He waited as Luther, Karin and Dino first checked and then slipped back into the embattled courtyard. The compound where the prisoners were kept lay to their left as they exited the building, which now presented a new predicament.

How could they cross the courtyard without getting shot?

Alicia spoke up when he stated the question. "We do what we do best," she said. "We cause total fucking chaos."

It sounded perfect to Drake.

CHAPTER THIRTY THREE

Dahl raced down into darkness, treading the worn concrete steps as fast as he dared, desperate to find and stop the bomb. He had no idea what he'd find below, nor how well it would be guarded, but only darkness pooled ahead and, unless his enemies were equipped with night-vision, they would all be equally blind.

Kenzie was a step behind, followed by Dallas and Molokai. The light they cast with their flashlights illuminated about four steps. Dahl followed a winding route down and down until he hit the very bottom.

"I'm at the bottom," he said.

Quickly, they assembled and swept the room for enemies, but found none. Dahl wasn't surprised. The Devil didn't strike him as the trusting type.

The Geiger counter was squealing so loudly that Dahl turned it off. The radiation level remained within acceptable levels, but it was moving closer to the red line. Molokai passed him to the right as his flashlight illuminated a niche in the wall.

"Got it."

Dahl gritted his teeth. All this time he'd been harboring a quiet hope that there was no real bomb. Just a ball of plutonium maybe. It would have made their journey off this island more comfortable and he was more than ready to get the hell off this island.

And back to his family in DC.

"Got pliers?" Molokai asked.

Dahl moved behind Kenzie and unfastened her backpack. He reached inside for its toolkit and extracted a pair of pliers. He handed them to Molokai as he peered over the big man's shoulder.

"You do know what you're doing, right?"

"I'm betting I know more than you."

"That's not reassuring at all."

Dahl saw a black steel casing sheathed in what appeared to be thick polystyrene. At one end of the casing, a flashing digital timer showed the numbers in blood-red. There was no keypad.

"Two and a half hours to detonation," Kenzie said. "C'mon, boys, it's getting real."

Dahl knew what she meant. When you knew a bomb was going to detonate in six hours, depending where you were, the urgency wasn't immediate. But as those hours counted down it quickly started to mount.

Molokai prized the casing apart with the pliers. Dahl bit his lip, wincing slightly. He saw wires exposed. Blues and yellows, reds and browns, a hot mass of color all twisted around each other. He saw a small dial that looked like a compass, and a pair of ends that appeared to be crocodile clips.

He barely breathed as Molokai picked among the wires with his pliers.

"One hundred and forty five minutes," Kenzie said.

Molokai paused, pliers poised around a single blue wire. "Please stay silent."

Dahl watched him close the pliers. Gently, he rested a hand on the man's arm. "How do you know that's the right one?"

Again, Molokai paused. He let out a long, deep breath before speaking. "Do you want us to blow up?"

"Not really, no."

"When you touched my arm I almost clipped this wire. This isn't the wire I want to clip. I'm moving it out of the way. If I clip this wire—we explode. Okay?"

Dahl cleared his throat nervously. "Okay."

"Maybe you should have packed your sledge hammer," Kenzie whispered in his ear.

Even here, Dahl shivered from the closeness of her lips, the sound of her breathy voice. It was quite a contrast to the scene in front of his eyes. Molokai eased the blue wire out of the way, so that he could reach the black wire.

Dahl was about to repeat his question, but gritted his teeth, keeping his mouth shut. Kenzie's grip on his shoulder grew tight, painful. Dallas, holding the main flashlight, could barely keep it still. This wasn't anything they'd ever been trained for. Yes, they'd defused a nuke before under desperate circumstances, but this was entirely different.

Also, it didn't need to be done. Molokai was taking a chance. Molokai was still mostly a mystery man. There was time to think, time to plan if they left the nuke alone. And if this was the wrong wire . . .

Molokai snipped, and Dahl momentarily closed his eyes. Right after it, he heard a terrifying dull click. When fire and death didn't consume him, he managed to look at the bomb. Nothing had changed.

Molokai was frowning at the device. "Ah, shit."

"What the fuck does that mean?"

"It means it didn't work. It means . . . run!"

"No, no." Kenzie stopped them. "You haven't kick started the bomb. You've sped up the timer."

Dahl glanced at it. There were now only one hundred and twenty minutes remaining.

"Whatever you do," he told Molokai. "Don't cut any more wires."

* * *

Drake fired on full auto as he ran with the others arrayed around him. Bullets shredded the old van and made it shudder. A moment later it exploded, flames licking the castle walls and shooting up into the air. Men, guns and metal flew to left and right, striking other men. The SPEAR team raced for the gap in the eastern wall that led to the beach, covering each other from front and rear.

It was a double formation. Drake, Hayden and Kinimaka at the front; Alicia, Luther and Karin at the back; Dino and Mai at the side, all firing at everything that moved. They made it to the gap and took cover behind the castle wall, their backs to thick concrete.

Drake pressed the comms. "Moving to the left. Cover me."

A compound lay that way, its tall wooden railings lashed together with stout rope, its gates secured with a heavy padlock. Behind the bamboo bars stood many figures. They knew what was going to happen to the island, but they had no way of knowing when, and no means of escape. Psychological torture had never been a problem for the Devil.

Drake ran freely, covered by his team. Alicia was at his side. To the right, a stretch of sandy beach led to the foaming ocean where dark breakers crashed over a reef and onto the island. Further still was the long, wide dock and jetty, made up of heavy planks and pillars of wood. Dinghies and Zodiacs, speedboats, motor launches and even rowing boats were tied up along the dockside, presumably awaiting their human cargo. There was a relatively smooth wooden path that cut along the beach from the castle and led to the docks, no doubt built to make moving heavy objects easier from ship to shore. This path was full of fighting men. There was close-quarter combat and gunfire, the clash of knives, the incredible sight of men making space to fire bows and arrows.

Drake checked the padlock then looked through the bars. "Get back."

A few seconds later he used a crowbar from his pack to break the lock. He rushed inside. Many faces greeted him, all of them wary. People just backed away.

"Are you here against your will?" he asked. "If so, come with us. We can save you."

"I am." A man came forward, hunched and grimacing in pain as if his back had been damaged.

"And me," a dark-haired woman said.

"And us." A young woman and a child came forward, making Drake grimace. He hadn't realized there were children here.

"How many are you?" he asked.

All the captives came forward into the light, grouping close to the center of the compound. They all looked frighteningly similar to Drake. Ragged and disordered. White faced and drawn. Lacking any sign of spirit. They shuffled as close as they dared, keeping a close guard on their neighbors and on their children.

Drake counted eighteen adults and three children. Of the eighteen six were women, one he would consider over sixty, and twelve were men, three he would consider over sixty. It would be a tough bunch to bear to safety.

This changed everything. He checked his watch. Less than two hours to go before the nuke exploded. The docks and the castle and even the beach were still crammed with fighting men. He could see the lights of the ships in the harbor, but only four vessels remained.

What the hell are we going to do?

Hopefully, Dahl would have had some luck defusing the bomb.

His comms crackled. They had managed to repair two of the comms before the team split. He was pleased to hear the big Swede's voice. "We're on our way. Requesting cover at the keep."

Drake keyed his comms. "Did you disarm it?"

"No. We actually brought the clock forward, so we have less time now."

Bollocks. "We're on our way with cover," Drake said. "But we have an even bigger problem here."

"Bloody hell, what's that?"

"Twenty one civilians, three of whom are kids."

Dahl was silent for a long moment.

Kenzie came back quickly as her distrustful side spoke up. "Make sure they're all civilians and not enemy plants," she said. "Get them apart and talk to them one on one. Do it quick."

Drake was glad once again for the Israeli's presence. It was a sound idea. He gave the order and left Hayden, Kinimaka, Karin and Dino behind to start the conversation.

"Wait at the keep door," he said. "We're coming for you."

CHAPTER THIRTY FOUR

They shepherded Dahl and the others across the courtyard and to the compound before taking stock by its broken gates.

"Ideas?" Hayden asked.

Luther used his rifle to point toward the docks. "There's only one boat that can take all of us. That motor launch. And I'm betting it's the Devil's."

"So it's a balls-out, blood and guts run for it?" Alicia questioned. "Typical Luther."

"You got a better idea?"

"No, but how do we protect the prisoners?"

"The big boys will attack," Luther said. "Me. Mai. Molokai. Drake. Dahl. Kinimaka. You and Kenzie. The others will be their bodyguards."

"I can't tell if that's a compliment or an insult, but I say hell yeah,"

"I'll stay with the prisoners," Mai said. "They may need a blood warrior too."

Drake thought it over. If there was another way, he couldn't come up with it right now. They could swim, but in the dark, with these waves, and then trying to haul everyone aboard the launch, they were bound to lose people.

Dahl was the first to step forward. "I agree with Luther. Let's get on with it."

Hayden waited as Molokai and Dino fired a volley at three Creepers intent on coming their way. All three attackers decided to turn and join the dock battle where it was easier to get involved.

"Time's short," Hayden said. "We don't have a choice. Make ready."

Within three minutes they were prepared to go. Drake watched as Hayden and Mai rounded up the prisoners, herding them into a tight group and handing out energy bars and water. It didn't take long.

"This is the fight of your lives," he heard Hayden tell them. "The hardest and hopefully best run you will all ever make. It should lead to freedom. Are you ready for it?"

There was a faint chorus of affirmations. Drake was buoyed to see fresh hope on their faces now that they were surrounded by a military team intent on their safety. He switched his attention to the front. Mercenaries had already jumped into one of the speedboats but were being swamped as several Hunters tried to join them. Men fell into the water and battled on deck. The boat pitched and heaved. The main crowd of fighters moved toward the head of the jetty.

The motor launch was moored just beyond this pack of fighters and to the right.

Drake nodded at Dahl and Alicia and then prepared himself mentally for what was about to happen. Together, they made a truly formidable team.

"Now!" Luther shouted.

They started forward at a fast jog. There were no innocents in front of them, only savage islanders and mercenaries battling for superiority. Running in a seven-strong wedge with Luther at the head, the SPEAR vanguard moved along the pathway toward the docks. As they approached the first enemy pack they opened fire.

Men fell away to left and right, sprawling onto the beach, leaving blood in the sand. Others tried to turn, to fire over their shoulders, but weren't quick enough. Drake kicked a wounded man in the face as he rushed by, fired two shots into another. They couldn't risk leaving too many alive to face off against the following prisoners. The wooden planks bent beneath their weight. The sound of their boots pounding along was an ominous death knell to all those that heard.

Drake had positioned himself next to the tip of the sword. Luther was formidable at the front, ducked low behind his gun and firing to left and right. Men fell everywhere, and those that fell in their path were shot again.

Ahead, those battling along the length of the docks seemed to sense the new danger. Many turned, pausing in their fight. Some started to run away; others started to run back. Many more chose to continue their battle. Drake shot three men in succession as he gained the docks, then shoulder barged another man through the nearby rail and into the ocean shallows. Their wedge smashed into a tight knot of fighting men.

And stalled.

With no forward momentum, the prisoners and their new guards would be left milling a few steps behind, easy targets. To pull this off and gain the launch, Drake knew they had to keep moving. Luther smashed to left and right, using his gun in one hand and his knife in the other. Where possible he used elbows too. Drake loosed bullet after bullet but found he was having to push and kick people out of the way, even those he'd shot. The sheer crush of numbers blocked the docks.

Slowly, they advanced.

Drake glanced back. Mai and the others were twenty steps behind. The Japanese woman and the remainder of the SPEAR team had formed a protective cordon around the prisoners and were herding them along. Mai killed a wounded man who raised his pistol, and Dallas killed another. Karin was forced into a few seconds of hand-to-hand with a Creeper wielding a knife, but managed to keep her position in line.

Drake saw they were halfway along the docks. The motor launch lay thirty feet up and to the right. There was no clear path. Men were battling on the edge of the wooden platform, falling into the water or leaping into boats. Engines roared. The bright silver moon cast a shimmering spotlight over it all, a contrast to the glaring floodlights that bathed the dock in a faint, hideous yellow. Drake heaved a man over the side, came so close to the edge that he toppled toward the sea himself, and felt a hand pulling him back.

"Steady," Dahl said.

Drake nodded. "Cheers, mate."

Bullets flew. A large gang of men turned and came at them, brandishing every weapon Drake could imagine. An axe flew end over end toward his scalp. He cried out a warning and ducked, heard the weapon's hissing passage overhead.

A man leaped in holding a spear, bringing it down hard as he landed. Alicia defended the attack and swept the man away over the other side of the docks, straight into the side of a waiting boat.

Drake fired into the attacking mass, seeing blood flow and men collapse, felling other men. Luther leapt up onto the backs of the fallen, using them to gain height and fire down at those behind. The pile shifted, but he kept his balance. Drake joined him on the right and Dahl to the left.

"We're almost there," the Swede said.

* * *

Behind, Mai kept her concentration, fully aware she was the leader of this pack. The prisoners were quiet for the most part, huddled and scared but game to keep moving. They could see how hard their rescuers were trying. Mai watched carefully, identifying those that were wounded and those that were dead. She saw their weapons and whether they intended to use them. Twice she saved the pack ahead from men who'd feigned injury, only to rise and try to attack from behind.

Others emerged from the surf to her right, weapons aimed. She picked them off one by one. She forced herself to take her eyes and mind off Luther, because she was too worried for his safety. Such concerns couldn't help her at this point, and they wouldn't help him either.

But the biggest threat, resulting in the greatest heroics, came from the left. Mai turned from a kill to see two Creepers standing in the rolling sea, their bows stretched taut, arrows knocked. There was no way to stop them firing.

She brought her gun around just a second too late. The arrows flew, quivering through the air, aimed for the center mass of the prisoners where the children were. Dread gripped her stomach, making her heart sink. There was no stopping those arrows and not everyone had seen them coming.

But Karin had. She backpedalled, instinctively knowing that there was only one option. She dragged Dino with her. Grimacing, the two shared a brief glance and then barged backward among the prisoners so that they took both descending arrows full in the chest.

The impact knocked them to the ground. The moving mass ground to a temporary halt as Dallas and Hayden reached down to first check and then haul them upright.

Their flak vests had done the work. They were bruised,

shocked, but very much alive. Mai dispatched both Creepers before they could cause any more issues and ordered them forward.

They couldn't stop moving.

Their lives depended on it.

Drake jumped down feet first from the pile of men, boots striking the face of an attacker. At the same time, he fired twice, hitting two hulking mercs. They fell to their knees, but it took two more shots from Molokai to finish them. Drake climbed to his feet. Luther was forging ahead, a bit too fast. Men were coming in behind him. Drake leapt to meet them, backed by Molokai and Kinimaka. Together they forced their way back to Luther's side, heaving at and stabbing and shooting the men in between. There was a good gap to the left which meant Mai and the prisoners wouldn't have to clamber over the pile of bodies.

To the right, the motor launch sat tied to the docks.

There was a small space around its boarding plank. Beyond that, a final large group of ex-soldiers and islanders still fought. There were more free boats at the end of the dock, which had drawn more men.

Luther ran to a short plank of wood that led aboard the launch. It was free. Drake thought it odd as he approached, flanked by Dahl and Kenzie. The launch itself was deserted and dark.

"Wait, brother," Molokai said. "This doesn't feel right."

Luther halted at the edge of the dock, hand on the rail, staring at the dark launch as if he could penetrate its secrets.

Kinimaka and Alicia made a temporary guard in front, warding off several islanders seeking to launch an attack.

Behind, Mai and the others were coming, just a dozen steps away.

Now what? Drake thought.

He didn't have long to wait.

From out of the mass of battling men at the end of the dock, stepping through their blood, broken bones and severed limbs, their bullet-shattered bodies, came the Devil himself, dripping crimson, carrying knives the size of rifles and grinning with a hard, feral insanity that sent a bolt of fear shooting through even the bravest of hearts.

CHAPTER THIRTY FIVE

The Devil was tall, taller even than Luther and Molokai, but well-proportioned for he had the muscular physique to match. He'd be an intimidating man even without the coating of other men's fresh blood. His face was angular and white; he appeared to be of Eastern European origin. His head was bald. He carried himself with the confidence and disdain of a man that expected to be obeyed.

"Lie down on your stomachs," the Devil said in a voice lacking any trace of an accent. "So that I can slit your throats."

With a snap of his wrist he flicked gore from the blade of his knife in their direction. Drake heard some splatter his vest but didn't look down. The Devil advanced a step, giving eight burly mercs the chance to squeeze past him and aim their weapons.

A pocket of quiet enveloped them.

"That isn't gonna happen," Drake said.

"It will. One day."

"Say—" Alicia waved her rifle "—can we see your horns?"

"Mock all you like, but you will rue the day you met the Devil. You will regret ever hearing my name. You know what I can do."

Drake knew, and so did the rest of the SPEAR team. He was aware of Mai only just a few steps away from them now, leading her wards at a slow pace.

"You've been spending too much time with Kovalenko," Dahl said. "You're starting to sound like him."

The Devil spat blood onto the wooden planks. "He is a walking dead man too. He should never have crossed the Devil."

Drake stared into those soulless eyes and saw how the man had earned his name. "Then tell me this . . . why the hell are you nuking this island?"

"Because Kovalenko got inside my head!" came the hissed reply. "Convinced me it would be a good idea. I'll tell you this . . . the nuke is to cover up the most terrible deed the Blood King has ever done, the most terrible deed a man can do. On this island he made scientists break down a large lump of plutonium stolen from an abandoned base in Chechnya. Once done, they made him twenty low-yield nuclear bombs."

Dahl gasped. Alicia spoke for all of them. "Are you fucking crazy? He could blight the world with those."

"I don't think he has intentions of using them. Or so he says. They're more insurance, or for a future project. Well . . . now that I've got all that off my chest, shall we fight?"

"Why are you telling us this?" Luther asked. "Here. Now."

"Because I am a pragmatist and, one way or another, I want the Blood King to suffer."

Mai came alongside. She didn't stop, just walked straight up to the bloodied man and stared him right in the eye.

"Run," she whispered. "Run away, now. Because if I get the chance I am going to send you straight down to fucking Hell."

The huddled, terrified prisoners at her back formed the foundation of her moral anger.

The Devil backed away and ran a hand over his bald scalp. "You know what I can do?"

Mai dropped her rifle and raised her knife so that it was

inches from his throat. "You come near my family, or the families of anyone I care for, ever again, and I'll make you wish you'd never heard my name."

Shouts sprang up from the crowd of prisoners. Mai's words were galvanizing them. Luther unhooked the chain that blocked their way to the motor launch.

The Devil cleared his throat. "That's my boat. Why do you think it's still here?"

"I don't see you on it," Alicia came right back.

Drake rolled his eyes. "Are we gonna fight, or what?"

"I was just doing that," the Devil said. "For fun, when you showed up and looked like you were about to steal my ride. Now I'm gonna kill you all. Oh, and you . . ." He glanced around Mai, straight at Dahl. "I'll be seeing you soon."

He kicked out at Mai. She caught the blow and twisted to the side, letting it fly past. The Devil's eight mercs sprang into action, launching themselves at Alicia and Kinimaka and anyone else standing in the front line. Blows were rained down and blocked. Other blows found their targets. Knives flashed. A spiked Kevlar wristband smashed Kenzie across the temple, sending her to her knees, stunned. Dallas stepped in, grabbed the wrist and struck it with an elbow. The merc screamed as the arm broke. Kenzie shook her head, dazed.

"We can't let them take control of the boat," Dahl grated to all those around him. "It's the only way to get everyone off this bloody island."

"Speaking of that," Drake said. "One hour until the explosion."

And then they were in the thick of it, holding off the Devil's mercs and trying to protect the prisoners from other factions cramming the length of the dock. It was a wild melee; a twisting, turning, frantic mix of hand-to-hand fighting, watching out for deadly missiles and keeping control of their part of the dock.

The prisoners huddled close to the rail. Dahl and Drake and others formed a half circle around them. Mercenaries attacked, breaking against the defense, falling dead or crawling away. Arrows were loosed and taken on bulletproof vests or evaded. Alicia and Hayden fell, gasping. Karin picked up Dallas.

They stood together and fought as one, shooting islanders and mercs when they could, punching and stabbing them when they couldn't. It was a pitched battle under the bright silver moon. It was against a ticking clock and oncoming certain death. It was a race against time before the ships' captains decided to set sail.

The Devil came at them with both knives and, when he lost those, continued with a rifle with a deadly bayonet attached. The bayonet was off-putting and he used it like nothing Drake had ever seen. It stabbed and swept and defended. It was thrust and then sliced at an angle.

First Mai confronted him, but was swept to the side by a large merc. Next, Drake came up against him. The Devil didn't land blows—every attack was designed to be a final kill. Every feint and parry lead to a deadly blow. He was unorthodox, surprising. Drake struggled. He took hard thrusts to the stomach and a slice to the arm. He staggered to the left.

Dahl took over.

But there was no beating the Devil back. He stood his ground and fought in that wild, unconventional manner. Dahl was looking heated enough to simply charge him when Luther gave a shout.

"Go, go, go!"

The prisoners swarmed across the plank of wood leading to the motor launch. They fled over one at a time and, thankfully, several of the men leapt toward the cabin to find the starter motor.

Four of the Devil's big mercs were down, four others were fighting like demons. These were professional special ops soldiers, handpicked for their expertise; far from the usual fodder the SPEAR team encountered. Molokai struggled with one whilst Kinimaka stumbled to and fro with another, both men clasping each other in a bear hug that was anything but placid.

Dahl backed away from the Devil. A swarm of islanders came from the dock's far side then, smashing into the Devil and the SPEAR team alike. Everyone staggered, fell or went down to their knees. Bodies passed over and above them or fell alongside. Some tried to jump on the plank and reach the motor launch, but Mai and Alicia were up fast enough to pick them off with well-placed shots.

All the prisoners were on board. The engine fired up. Lights came on, flooding the deck. Mai and Alicia stood sentry at the entrance to the boarding gate, soon joined by Dino and Karin.

"Move!" Alicia shouted, raising her rifle.

Drake didn't wait. The four shooters had control of the battle and the situation. He trusted them. He turned his back on the fight and fled to the launch, hitting the plank and running on board. Feet pounded at his back and he was ready for an enemy, but when he whirled, knife ready, he saw Dahl then Luther.

Together, they lined the back of the launch, guns targeted, covering everyone else's headlong charge onto the big boat. The Devil glared at them through a mask of blood, his lips tightly sealed. Only three big mercs still guarded him and they tried to pull him away.

Five other boats remained around the docks, the rest were pounding through the crashing waves toward their ships. Mai was last aboard the launch, skidding as she hit the boards of the deck. Drake shoved off the plank they had used as a walkway and Luther bellowed out an order to start moving.

Behind, the dock still surged with men, but it was a more localized struggle now. Just two packs, mostly made up of Creepers and Hunters, fighting for the last three boats. Still, arrows shot toward them and a spear crashed into the side of their boat, sinking in and vibrating loudly. Shots were fired. Everyone dove to the deck.

Drake crawled to the side, where he could peer out and see what the Devil was up to.

Alicia rested her head on his shoulder. "What do you see, Drakey?"

He smiled, happy she was at his side. They were breathing heavily, unable to tell which whorls of blood came from their own seeping wounds. They were both still shocked at everything that had happened today. All they had seen. And all they had left behind.

"He's commandeered one of the speedboats. Just him and his three goons. The bastard's already on his way to freedom."

"The last man we need roaming the world," Alicia said.

"You can bet your ass one of those goons is Grant Hawkins," Hayden said. "The inside man Tolley told us about. If the devil gets away, Hawkins will be useful."

"With the devil and Kovalenko free, we're gonna need all the help we can get." Dahl said.

Mai fell in beside them, checking her watch. "Forty nine minutes," she said. "We're going to have to speed up in order to reach safe distance."

CHAPTER THIRTY SIX

As their launch drew away from the brightly lit dock area, everyone stood close and stared in silence. The sights that met their eyes were stunning to behold. From the end of the dock to the beach, men fought, apparently unable to break free from their combat to flee. What remained of the Scavenger clan stalked the prisoner's compound and the keep, dragging two enemies along with them by the hair.

Fires burned. The top floor of the keep was in flames. The sandy beach was a churned mass of yellow grit and blood. Shouts and screams of desperation filled the air but no quarter was given. Clansmen even ran back, away from the boats, to end feuds with their enemies. Weapons rose and fell everywhere. Gunshots still rang out.

The sound of speedboats roaring brought their gazes to the waiting flotilla of ships.

Drake cursed. Only two remained. The Devil was arrowing toward one whilst a boat full of fighting men bounced chaotically toward the other. Two other ships had departed not so long ago—he could see their lights bouncing up and down in the distance as they plowed through the high seas.

Men aboard dinghies and small rafts paddled with their hands, hoping to reach a safe distance. On others all lay dead as if they'd engaged in ritual suicide. Drake knew they'd probably been picked off by sharp shooters.

Their own craft smashed through the center of a bobbing dinghy, sending plumes of water and three men high into the air. There were dozens of figures in the water too, striking out for some distant shore. Drake couldn't imagine where they would go. Guam was a long way from here.

The island with its irregular shores and cliffs, its mountains and trees, grew smaller but more identifiable as they motored away. The high mountain towered over it all, keeping its terrible secrets forever now, it seemed. Nobody would ever know what had happened to the poor creatures who lived up there.

Without evidence, without proof, it was only one more word-of-mouth indictment of the Devil himself.

Drake checked the countdown. "Thirty eight minutes," he said. "Most of those guys aren't gonna make it."

Everyone crowded closer around the stern of the boat. Molokai, Luther and Kinimaka walked to the raised prow, where they could see just as well and help offset the balance. The SPEAR team took those moments to relax, recharge and give thanks that they had survived. Mai crossed to Luther's side. Dino stayed close to Karin. Not only had it been a tough battle up the mountain for them, it had been an arduous voyage in a container across the ocean too. This then, was their first real breath of freedom.

Hayden and Kinimaka sat together, one in front of the other. In the stillness, Drake felt the pain of a dozen throbbing wounds. A shot of penicillin was probably in order too.

"How long?" Hayden asked.

"Thirty five minutes," Drake said. "Are we at safe distance yet?"

"No way, we're gonna have to get moving." Hayden turned to shout at the pilots.

Then it happened. Nobody had thought that the timer might have sped up or skipped forward more than once after Molokai's botched attempt to disarm it, but clearly it had.

There was a devastating precursor flash, which made everyone on board the launch spin away. Then there came a white hot, searing explosion of light, something that turned the backs of their eyelids a bright red for several long, terrifying seconds. As the flash died away, the rumbling began. It built to a crescendo; an echoing, thundering, resounding explosion that might have been the entire earth moving. It came in waves, crashing over the boat and all those on board.

Drake slammed his hands to his ears, looking to the island now that the initial explosive light had vanished. The noise was so great that it was like a physical force slamming against his eyeballs. His skin rippled, his lips were dry as bone. A reverberating, crashing din was all he knew. Light still covered the island, plumes and plumes of it burgeoning out. It was too bright, hurting his eyes. The thunder crashed by and the light swelled, glowing clouds burgeoning from the point of the explosion.

It was everything. It was all they could see, hear and think about. It saturated their senses so completely they knew nothing else.

Then it was gone.

Drake gasped and fell to the deck. The clouds mushroomed upward. The shockwave would come next and then the fallout. If they weren't far enough away they'd be killed. He looked up to see the blast of air spreading out from the island. It churned the beach into ash. It chopped the waves into foam and flurry. It skimmed the ocean, an unstoppable force.

"Down!"

Drake grabbed Alicia and pulled her under his body,

sheltering her as best he could. He knew the rest of the SPEAR team would be doing more or less the same. He saw one of the children peering from underneath her mother's chest, dark eyes full of fear.

The worst of it never came. The brunt of the shockwave petered out before striking the boat. A hot gust of wind did hit them, propelling the boat forward for about twenty feet, making the prow lift and skim across the rolling waters at high speed, but it died out as quickly as it came. Drake waited half a minute and then raised his head, staring back toward the island.

"Low yield," he said. "Thank God for that."

"I echo that sentiment," Alicia said. "Wholeheartedly."

Slowly, those aboard the boat sat up, happy to be alive. The two pilots grabbed the steering wheel and held on, one of them calling out to Luther for a course. More people rose, so long prisoners but now free and able to do as they pleased. It would be a long road to rehabilitation but at least they had the chance and the strength to start.

"I hope they make it," Drake said as Dahl walked up to them. "I can't imagine what they've been through."

"Those with younger children stand the best chance," Dahl said. "Because kids are resilient, and they can get you through anything."

"You hiding from Kenzie?" Alicia peered around him.

"Yeah, a little."

"Want me to chuck her overboard for you?"

Dahl peered at her. "I take back what I said about kids. Maybe they need an Alicia with them. You seem able to bounce back from anything."

"It's either that, Torsty, or maybe I present a cheery front so they can't see me crying inside."

Dahl grabbed her and hugged her close. "Stop being

soft," he said. "You know we all love you."

Drake watched the cloud expand up toward the atmosphere. There were sounds of happiness all around, claps on backs and handshakes.

But he knew, although they'd won this time, the battle was far from over.

CHAPTER THIRTY SEVEN

The motor launch sailed on into the dark ocean, guided by its own navigation and the twinkling stars above.

Hayden called the relevant authorities, delegating where she could. It wasn't long before the United States military was dispatching crafts and vessels from Guam.

"A couple of hours," Hayden reported to everyone. "Less probably, and we'll be rescued."

They kept an eye on the ocean, but no other crafts were visible through the gloomy dark. Trackers were left on so that their rescuers would be able to pinpoint their location. They drifted with the current, watching the radar and navigational instruments, but no dangers presented themselves. Soon, they had put Devil's Island to their stern.

Drake found he now had the time to share everything he'd wanted to whilst they were on the island. He hadn't seen Mai or Luther since they left for their meal back in London, and commended them for their incredible efforts since. They commiserated with each other over Lauren and Smyth but looked forward to visiting Yorgi. Karin had been gone longer and he'd never even met Dino. He talked briefly to them, learning how Karin had sought to infiltrate the Blood King's organization, and wondered how close she'd come to joining.

Maybe not close at all.

Then there were Kenzie and Dallas, the first of whom had quit the team before London, the second dragged along for the wild ride. He spoke to them and made it clear they were both welcome to stay with the team. Kenzie's eyes still strayed in Dahl's direction but didn't remain there for long.

They gathered around the stern, holding onto the brass handrail and gazing into the blackest of black nights. The only lights out there were vague reflections of the scattered stars and rolling wedges of silver moonlight.

"I hate it that the Devil escaped," Hayden said. "It's just another evil bastard out in the world."

"He's always been there," Kinimaka said. "Well, for the last few decades. I don't mean 'forever.'" He made a speech sign with the fingers of both hands. "Like he's the real king of the underworld or something."

His words lightened their mood. "The Blood King was initially on the island too," Mai said, looking around at them as if unsure what they knew. "I heard one of our captors mention him."

"Captors?" Alicia asked.

"It was a long voyage and then a very special guided tour through the caves," Luther told them. "There were quite a few underworld figures on this island when we arrived. Partying. Making deals. I guess they all left early."

"You recognize any of them?" Drake asked. It would be good to know who the Devil did his business with. It might help track him down, or at least they could put the sword to some of his contacts.

"No." Luther shook his head with regret. "But I would remember one of the yachts I saw out in the harbor that first morning. It was beautiful, dark chrome and as sleek as a woman's . . ." He paused, glancing at Mai uncertainly. ". . . well, it was pretty sleek. I'd know that boat anywhere."

"It's a good starting point," Hayden said. "But I do hate having to wait for Kovalenko to raise his ugly head again."

"Yeah, especially if he's got nukes," Dahl said.

They sobered. The seas rolled them to and fro. A calm and soothing wind swept past their faces, fresh and cool and laced with a little bit of sea spray. Drake studied the patches of silver cast by the moon.

"I guess that's the end then," he said, reflecting over all they had been through since London. "I mean, normally we raise a glass. Talk it through. Look forward. But this time it isn't so easy."

He saw sorrow in the future. Lauren and Smyth's funerals. The hunt for Yorgi's family. The funerals of the SAS soldiers who died for him. It was going to be a tough few days.

"But we do have each other," Alicia said as if reading his mind. "All of us, I mean. No member of the SPEAR team is ever alone."

"I think you've found our new motto." Drake shook the sadness away for a minute and put his arms around her. "Far better than Who Dares Wins."

"Not quite as catchy." Kenzie sat close behind them on a bulkhead. "It needs work."

"Things have changed," Hayden said in a low voice. "It will never be the same. Not only because of Lauren and Smyth—and Yorgi—but with the DC operation. The headquarters. Our role. The government hunted us. Sent a kill team after us—"

Luther coughed. "Sorry about that, folks."

Hayden went on. "They turned on us in a moment, after everything we've done. I know there was a rogue organization involved, but somebody should have fought for us, trusted us, had our backs."

"It's politics," Luther said.

"I know that. It's always politics. Power and influence, wealth and greed. Throw a team to the wolves to improve your standing, to cover something up, to make friends in low places. Whatever. I can't continue to work with that and I wonder if you can too?"

Her words stopped. A deep silence followed. Drake knew that she was about to offer up her proposition. It had been a long time coming.

"You have a game-changing idea," he said. "I know that. But can it wait one more day?"

Hayden inclined her head. "I guess. Why?"

"We have one more job to do."

CHAPTER THIRTY EIGHT

The next day, rested but still immensely tired, they landed in Russia. A transporter had lifted them from Guam and taken them to Europe where they debriefed before commandeering the first ride to Moscow. Drake couldn't work out how long it had been since he'd seen Yorgi, but it had been far too many months. Plus there'd been several recent hours when he'd thought Yorgi was gone forever.

The Russian air was biting cold and shot through with snow. They hadn't come prepared, and bore the brunt of it as they crossed airport tarmac to climb into waiting cars. At least it was warm inside.

As was normal in their lives these days, the hours passed with frightening similarity. A different town or city, a different country, it made no difference. It was all the same. Their lives passing them by.

But Drake's spirits were high during this journey. It took just an hour to drive from the airport to the hospital. Men were waiting for them near the doors; men with guns. They passed two more checkpoints on the way up to the third floor. One man then indicated a white door and said, "Take as long as you need."

They intended to. This was a poignant reunion.

Drake entered first. Yorgi was sitting up in bed, wearing a sky-blue T-shirt and flicking through a car magazine. His face creased into joy when he saw them, and he tried to climb out of the covers.

Drake hurried forward. "Stay right there, pal," he

ordered. "Don't wanna tear those stitches."

"Not only that," Alicia said, at his back. "We don't want any surprise glimpses of Little Yorgi, if you know what I mean."

"Hey," the Russian's face creased even deeper, "you called me by my real name."

"There's a first for everything. It won't happen again."

Drake shook hands with his old friend then leaned in for a hug. Alicia was next. The atmosphere was charged with excitement and happiness, undercut by more than a little sadness. Drake understood he had to stay right there in the moment, chatting and involved, to prevent the tears from blurring his eyes.

"Well done for surviving," Kinimaka told Yorgi. "We thought we'd lost you, bud."

"It wasn't just me," Yorgi said. "Actually, it wasn't really me at all. It was those outstanding soldiers Cambridge sent to watch over me at your request." He nodded at Drake.

"What were their names?" Alicia asked.

"Sean Webster and John Archer. Both bloody heroes." Yorgi's eyes misted over.

"Two more good men gone," Drake said, bowing his head.

"You found your family?" Hayden asked.

Yorgi looked up, sniffing. "I did. I marked them right before the attack. I guess I'm just waiting to heal before I head back out there."

"If you would allow us," Hayden said. "We can finish that for you."

She'd made a few phone calls on the flight over, organizing the tools and equipment and men they would need to finish the job as quickly as possible. Sonar would pinpoint the bodies and then ice-breaking equipment would get them close. Men would do the rest.

Yorgi looked hopeful. "You would help me put them to rest?"

"Of course." Drake punched him on the arm. "You're family, mate."

"Ow! But, don't you have another mission to start?"

Drake pulled up a chair. "This is our only mission now. This, and then some funerals back in DC. Are you up for it?"

"Oh God, of course. I want to be there."

"Then tell us about these trackers."

"They're just basic GPRS markers that send data back to a laptop." Yorgi pointed to a side table, where a black Sony lay with its top closed. "It's so simple even Alicia could follow it."

"Oy!"

Time passed. Hayden took the laptop, found the data, and sent it to the team waiting at the very hotel where Yorgi had been watched by Webster and Archer just a few days ago, before the new Blood King tried to wreak his vengeance on the President and London. Drake dwelled on it all and tried to ignore his throbbing bruises, his raw scrapes and cuts. He caught Yorgi's attention.

"What's the food like here?"

"I've eaten worse," Yorgi said. "But then I did spend years in prison."

"Let's order out," Kinimaka said, looking around the room anxiously. "I'm starving."

"There's no way we're going to the Hard Rock, Mano," Alicia said. "That's where we were when this thing started."

"I don't mind where we go," Kinimaka said. "As long as they do meat."

The team started to rise. Drake pointed at the bed covers. "You coming, mate? You decent under there or want us to turn around?"

"I'll throw some jeans on. No point turning around. Alicia's gonna look anyway."

"You know me so well." The blonde stared as Yorgi swung his legs out of bed. "Have to say, Yogi, I've seen smaller."

"I'm wearing pants, woman."

"Yeah, but a girl gets an eye for measurements once she's been around a few times. Isn't that right, Kenzie?"

The Israeli gave her the finger, but couldn't help smiling. Drake tried to tune it all out and brace himself for what was to come next. It would be one of the hardest days of his life. He spent a few moments taking stock of his team. They all looked bedraggled. Worn. That was it; the last few years had been an incredibly long ride. This particular chapter would end with the funeral of their friends.

It would be a heart-breaking but significant end.

And a sign that they all had to move on.

Washington DC's weather was little better than Moscow's. There was no snow, but the rain beat down at an unrelenting tempo. The streets were wet, slick, and looked fresh, almost new. The skies were gray, hanging low. It all suited the SPEAR team's mood as they walked under black umbrellas to the side of a double grave in a churchyard near Arlington National Cemetery. The only thing Drake heard was the steady drumming of rain on his umbrella. All he could see was water.

Not just rain.

Because they had no family, Lauren and Smyth could be buried side by side, as they'd died. They'd never be parted again. There were thirteen members of the SPEAR team present—its full remaining membership—and one thing was clear to them all.

As Team SPEAR, this was the last time they'd ever be together.

The rain fell, and with it the tears, and nothing would ever be the same again. Two lives were over, but thirteen more were changed irrevocably and forever. Drake remembered where he'd met Smyth—aboard the plane with Mai and Romero—and how Lauren had first come into their lives under the guidance of Jonathan Gates. The ceremony was short, and then they all came forward one by one, throwing a handful of soil down into the final resting place of their great friends.

"Never forget," Drake said. "And always move on."

"One life," Alicia said. "Live it with people you love."

It was a poignant take on her old motto. It was the change in Alicia, a change she was still coming to terms with.

Together, they stood as a team, one final time with Lauren and Smyth, bonded by hardship and trust, experience and friendship. SPEAR was a family that would live on long after it became a memory.

Once it was over, Drake moved to Yorgi's side. The two of them led the way to a different part of the cemetery, where the young Russian's brothers and sister were being buried. This time the ceremony was longer, as Yorgi spoke all the words he'd struggled to say for so long. Finally, though, he had closure. Finally, he'd laid them to rest properly, as they deserved. No longer would the memory of what his parents had done to his siblings weigh so heavy. He could do no more for them now.

There was one more deed to do on that chill, rainswept day. Sean Webster and John Archer had been flown back to the UK for burial, but Drake and the rest of the team joined Yorgi in several moments of silence to respect the deeds and deaths of two soldiers they'd have been proud to have on the team.

After that, as Drake said, it was off to the pub.

A shot of whiskey for each of the fallen, raised and downed at the bar. A wake that centered on them but involved everyone. A time to recall the best of memories and to laugh, a time to hope that one day they might all be reunited.

Religion didn't matter. What you believed didn't matter. An afterlife together was a soldier's, a friend's and a family's dearest hope.

CHAPTER THIRTY NINE

In sharp contrast, the next day dawned sunny and warm. The team ignored all calls except their own and agreed to meet for a late breakfast in a large restaurant close to Capitol Hill. They could see the Mall from their window, the wide stretch of grass that led from the Capitol building to the Washington Monument. The sunshine struck it dead center, making it feel like a breath of fresh air.

A tense expectancy hung over the entire team. It was time for Hayden's proposal. There was no downplaying this monumental moment in their lives. Drake knew and hoped it would shape their next steps and entire future. He'd been optimistic about it for what felt like a very long time.

As pancakes and maple syrup filled the table with a heady smell, as bacon, hash browns and an assortment of fruit and bread, jams and butter, arrived. As the coffee started to flow. As their lives turned and their futures hung in the balance, Hayden began to speak:

"To reiterate," she said, buttering toast. "No team can go on doing what we've done forever. No team should have to. I feel dejected when I see and hear about teams like ours ordered time and again into battle. Without thought. Without conscience. Without care for what they see and what they are forced to do. It hit me hard when the government turned on us. Until then, I didn't stop to think. It all seemed normal and I thought those in charge had our backs. But support, it seems, is conditional.

"When we met with undesirable events there was no

assistance, no help. Nobody risked their lives for us in our moment of need. Our wellbeing was of no consequence to them because they were off being self-serving, gratifying their own needs. They didn't recognize the goodness in our team, the service we've provided without question, even though we have fought and lost and died for them for years. I thought about all that and I thought something had to change. How can we continue doing what we love but under our terms? How can we decompress and re-energize between missions? How can we live personal lives and still save the world? Because, my friends, and you all know this, personal life should be warmer and more involving than the professional one. If we don't change, we will lose our chance of living."

Drake listened and ate at the same time. Hayden made a lot of sense. The food was good. The restaurant was warm and quiet. The breakfast crowd had come and gone, and it would be a while before the lunchtime gang arrived.

Hayden held up her knife to reinforce her next point. "I thought about this long and hard," she said. "This proposal will go straight to the President. We've earned that. I . . . well I'm a bit nervous about it now." She laughed.

"It's okay," Drake said. "We agree with you so far."

He saw it on all their faces; knew people like Luther and Molokai, seasoned soldiers, felt the same. Most military men danced to a politician's tune. It was disliked, but a man had to believe he was doing some good.

"It would go something like this," Hayden said with more authority. "We become the first of a brand-new kind of team. An innovative strike-force, whose remit is to come together only when the world is faced with the direst threat. Whatever that may be. Archaeological missions. Crazy world-killers like Kovalenko. Whatever."

"That's a little like what we do already," Dahl said.

"Not quite," Hayden said. "Because, at the moment, we chase whatever new threat we're told to chase. But in the future, we pick our mission, our way, our decision, our strategy. If it's not for us, and we all agree . . . we pass. Which brings me on to the second and best part of the proposal."

Drake watched as freshly cooked bacon was placed before him, zoning out for a moment. "Just how I like it."

Hayden snapped her fingers. "Stay with me. By sticking to this principle, by making this principle the core element of our team and impressing it on the hierarchy, we can all live normal lives for extended periods of time in between missions. We're not military and we're not private. We're a new unit. It wouldn't matter where we lived or who we lived with, so long as we all came together in the right place when we're called on. There are other teams capable of handling the admittedly important but not world-shattering stuff. We have earned the right to live, and choose our battles."

"Most of the pricks in Washington wouldn't go for it," Luther said, his voice filled with the weight of experience. "They'd say they're getting very little return for their money and there's no real accountability. Anything to further their own aims."

"Agreed," Hayden said. "But this is the President we're asking for help. Not Capitol Hill. And we're not lobbying. It's take it or leave it."

"Risky," Luther said.

"We risk it all every day. As a team, we're worth it. If we believe in ourselves we can pull it off."

"It's not like we're asking for more money or partying on the nation's expense sheet," Drake thought out loud. "And, don't forget the main focal point—we're still the tip of the sword, the first responders if there's a dire threat. And that very fact alone puts us in worse danger. And obviously we'll be first in when the Devil or the Blood King raise their heads again."

Hayden nodded, eating a mouthful of toast before continuing. "Everything you said there helps cement our argument."

"And a fresh new team is a strong team," Alicia put in. "It'd be nice to get shagged somewhere other than in a hotel room."

Dahl leaned over to Drake. "Careful, mate, that sounds like she's planning on buying a house."

Drake choked on a mouthful of coffee. "One step at a time, love. One step at a time."

"Can you stand a few months without me?" Alicia asked the room in general. "It'll be harder than you can imagine."

There were smiles, but Drake knew it would be tough at first. It was rare that he hadn't seen at least one of these faces every single day over the last five years. But time would give them all a chance to mend; it would give people like Dahl the chance to save their relationships. In short, it would provide them with a new, real life.

"Do it," Drake said. "I love the idea."

"There are a few issues to iron out," Hayden admitted. "We don't need a base, but we do need access to safe houses, armories, bank accounts and much more all over the world. And we need a signal."

Kinimaka cleared his throat eagerly. "Something they could shine in the sky?"

The whole table burst into laughter. It was a good moment, Drake thought. A place in the road where they branched off and headed toward better things. A turning point.

He thought about his life and all that he'd accomplished. Where it was impressive, it would be nothing without this team. As a man, he'd always wanted to help others but knew now that sometimes it couldn't be done. It could never be promised. He fought every day to better the lives of others, but there came a time when you had to take care of yourself and those you loved.

It would be an emotional future.

Alicia could finally stop running. She could put down some roots. Start fresh from a stable base. It was everything she needed, and Drake would be at her side every step of the way. For Dahl it was a new—and probably final—chance with Johanna. And the children needed their father at home.

Hayden and Kinimaka might finally admit their love, he thought, and start working on a way to prove it to each other. Too long, they'd skirted the issue and even purposely driven it away.

But now they could face it head on.

As for the others, he saw Kenzie running some kind of side business with Dallas. Hopefully, if she agreed to this new proposal which gave her the time she'd been wanting, she would stick with the team and the side business would be legal. Molokai and Luther were unknowns, but Drake knew the team wouldn't let them drift away or live alone. They'd be regular house guests for sure.

Luther was looking wistful even now. "I've always fancied an acting career," he said. "Maybe it's something I could pursue now. On the side." He grinned, a big man with a big presence and all the charisma in the world.

Karin and Dino would be around, Drake was sure. Maybe together. But they'd need some guidance. The commitment he'd felt toward Ben Blake continued in his love for Karin. He'd always be there for her.

Which left Mai Kitano. One of the loves of his life. A moral and worthy friend. The greatest, most dependable warrior he'd ever known. Mai had several choices and her future might be the most traveled of all of them. She might choose to take Luther with her. They seemed good together. It was certain she'd return to see Grace, whom she saw as a daughter, and Chika, her sister. The road had a long way to go for Mai Kitano—and held many more adventures.

So, Drake, there in the restaurant in the heart of America, surrounded by family, joined together by deep camaraderie, sat beside a woman he could see himself growing old with, looked forward to a brighter future and a new beginning. He saw days of rest and relaxation, of chilling out, of togetherness, forged and framed by new missions that would enable them all to keep doing that which they loved.

Maintaining the freedoms of the civilians of the world.

"You all want me to take this to the President?" Hayden asked.

Drake watched as everyone nodded. Even Kenzie was smiling, and Dahl looked about as relieved as a man given a second chance at life.

"Here's to the future," Hayden said, raising a mug of coffee.

"Here's to us," Drake said.

The new team started a new day.

CHAPTER FORTY

The Devil gripped a sidearm in his right hand and a radio in the other. He was hiding in a veritable rat's nest, surrounded by garbage and old boxes, rusted car parts and half-empty oil drums. This small garage had lain deserted for years, home to the odd derelict and layabout, overlooked by anybody that gave a damn, a festering eyesore that had never made anyone money and was therefore ignored.

The Devil's men had pinpointed it as a great location from which to strike. His faith in them was well placed. It sat toward the end of the parade route, where celebrations would be at their highest and most distracting, and where the furore would start.

He sat alone. He was the best the world had ever seen at this kind of thing. His only distraction, and the vicious topic that consumed his mind, was the betrayal of Luka Kovalenko. It made him want to quit the job, but pride told him otherwise. Nevertheless, he'd paid off the two men who'd helped facilitate this kill and sent them away. He'd be using them again soon. When he arrived in America his first directive was to ensure everything important went to the new home he was calling Devil's Junction. This included men, captives, arms and belongings. His second directive was to drive straight to Washington DC.

Interestingly, Torsten Dahl was here. In this city right now. He hadn't come home to visit his family yet. He was too intent on attending funerals and having late breakfasts. The Devil imagined he'd regret that.

Parade time.

Two miles east, it had already started. A peaceful group made up of families, supporters, friends, relatives and reporters was headed this way, ambling along in aid of the police retirement fund. It would take about thirty minutes for them to reach him. The Devil held two old, battered Glocks last used in DC three years ago as some part of convenience store raid. He carried a scarred knife that, according to police data, had been used only three months before to cut an officer before being confiscated. He carried spare bullets, old and untraceable. In addition, he also carried high-powered weapons in case he was forced to flee. It hadn't happened in two decades, but the Devil always came prepared.

Already, he could hear the music. Not long now. In the lull, Kovalenko again harried at his mind. *He'll regret leaving me to die in nuclear fire. My revenge will be more than fitting.*

He looked forward to beginning the planning of it tomorrow.

The street right across the road led to a needy neighborhood. The young men of that neighborhood had been stoked and riled during the previous few nights. One of their number had been beaten up by a man in a police uniform. Shots had been fired. The real police assured them it wasn't one of their own. Unforgiving fires had been lit. Perhaps they weren't on the verge of murder and mayhem yet, but the Devil knew a bunch of them would come protesting; they'd come angry, and if one more of their number was hurt unjustly they would start a riot.

He pulled at the shirt of the cop's uniform he wore. It was a little tight.

Confident in his own abilities, he would then melt away

and merge with the crowd where, minutes later, shots would ring out. Who would be killed?

Just three.

Job done.

The Devil saw the first faces come into view. The parade was approaching. He'd already had confirmation that Johanna Dahl and her girls were present. It was time to move.

Rising, he skulked back through the garage, avoiding pools of oil and debris until he reached a dilapidated doorway. Morning sunshine slanted in, bathing his face. He loitered for just a few minutes as the parade leaders drew level. That was the time to move.

Lowering his cap, he walked out into the open—the Devil abroad and making mayhem in DC—and headed for the right flank of the parade. It was loud. Many were singing along to a tune being pumped through two loudspeakers bluetoothed to a slow-moving car's playlist. Real police officers were in evidence, scattered along the route, and the Devil pinpointed all their positions now.

Nothing to worry about. The parade was passing the street he'd marked earlier, and there came the protesters. Right on time. A larger group than he'd imagined, than he'd been warned about. A feeling of euphoria filled him. This was living, this was the dream he'd always pursued. He was the man, the myth, the legend. Those in the world who knew he existed feared ever hearing his name.

He crossed the sidewalk, walked into the road and pushed through the men and women forming the parade. They were happy to let him by. They wore generic bright yellow T-shirts with similar slogans and hooded jackets and jeans and shorts. They were normal people; the type he detested. They grinned and clapped him on the back, tried to shake his hand. The Devil drew away from it all. Human contact wasn't his forte. He didn't want to be infected with their desperation, their morbid fantasies and moody tastes. He found space and exited the far side, now facing the oncoming protestors.

He made a show of holding up a hand, moving his lips as if speaking. There was no sound coming out. They passed him, some giving him an odd look. It didn't matter. Minutes passed. The protestors stopped short of the parade, shouting loudly, adding their voices to the din. The Devil glanced back, catching sight of Johanna almost exactly where he'd been told she would be.

Engage final attack.

It would have to be fast and precise. And it was. The Devil slipped a Glock from underneath his left armpit, holding it inside his jacket for just a moment before yelling: "Police, stop!"

Protestors looked around, most in surprise. The Devil held up the handgun and fired one shot in the air and then one shot into the stomach of a young man. The man folded, hands going to his chest where a spot of blood bloomed. The Devil threw the gun to the floor then smashed two more people across the face before running into the heart of the parade goers and shrugging his police jacket to the floor.

He threw his cap away. Now he wore the same T-shirt as three hundred parade goers. He slipped through them, heading for the center. A terrible commotion had begun to the right as people tried to find him, chase him down, as they screamed in protest, as they looked for someone to take their anger out on. All they had seen was a cop shooting one of their own. Now they saw the parade goers possibly protecting that cop. The shouts grew angry, full of hatred. Real cops were darting into action.

The Devil was still acting fast. Less than a minute had passed since he fired. Already, he had Johanna and her two kids in sight. He came up swiftly behind them.

Slipped the other Glock out.

Torsten Dahl would kill himself when he found out what had happened here, and how close he had been to it all.

The Devil kept his gun under his jacket. Necks were craning to the right. Police were threading through the crowd, looking for the source of the upheaval. Other men and women were looking for the shooter. He didn't reveal his gun again, just came right up to Johanna's back.

She turned as he pulled the trigger, her face open and questioning. Her two girls were close, so close he could have touched them on the tops of their heads, so close just the slightest turn of the barrel would line them up in his sights.

"Are you okay?" Johanna started to ask.

It was right then that the face of Luka Kovalenko once more smashed to the forefront of his mind. The Blood King's face replaced Johanna's, and, for a few moments, it was all he could see. Pure hatred flooded his veins, making his blood run cold. The Devil was all but consumed with the need for vengeance.

"Hey, sir, are you okay?" Johanna asked again.

The Devil realized only now that he hadn't finished pulling the trigger. It was still at three-quarter draw. With just a flick he could end this woman's life.

But the Blood King still hovered before his mind's eye. This was the job Kovalenko wanted him to do.

To hell with pride. To hell with an unblemished kill record. To hell with everything that Kovalenko wanted. This woman and her children will live, and that reflects on his arrogance, not mine.

Smiling into her blue eyes, he leaned forward.

"Tell your husband that you came face to face with the Devil," he said. "And that you're the first person in history whom I let live."

Ignoring her fear, her shock, he stole away through the back of the parade, pleased with himself and with the plans he had for the future.

THE END

For more information on the future of the Matt Drake world and other David Leadbeater novels please read on:

Another exciting book comes to an end and, I hope, leaves an interesting premise on which to start the next chapter of the constantly evolving Matt Drake series. The new phase will begin with Book 21. I'm looking at releasing Relic Hunters 3, already written, in May 2019 and, just a few months later, the next Drake, which I'm currently planning and eager to get stuck into.

If you enjoyed this book, please leave a review.

Other Books by David Leadbeater:

The Matt Drake Series
A constantly evolving, action-packed romp based in the escapist action-adventure genre:

The Bones of Odin (Matt Drake #1)
The Blood King Conspiracy (Matt Drake #2)
The Gates of Hell (Matt Drake 3)
The Tomb of the Gods (Matt Drake #4)
Brothers in Arms (Matt Drake #5)
The Swords of Babylon (Matt Drake #6)
Blood Vengeance (Matt Drake #7)
Last Man Standing (Matt Drake #8)
The Plagues of Pandora (Matt Drake #9)
The Lost Kingdom (Matt Drake #10)
The Ghost Ships of Arizona (Matt Drake #11)
The Last Bazaar (Matt Drake #12)
The Edge of Armageddon (Matt Drake #13)
The Treasures of Saint Germain (Matt Drake #14)
Inca Kings (Matt Drake #15)
The Four Corners of the Earth (Matt Drake #16)
The Seven Seals of Egypt (Matt Drake #17)
Weapons of the Gods (Matt Drake #18)
The Blood King Legacy (Matt Drake #19)

The Alicia Myles Series
Aztec Gold (Alicia Myles #1)
Crusader's Gold (Alicia Myles #2)
Caribbean Gold (Alicia Myles #3)

The Torsten Dahl Thriller Series
Stand Your Ground (Dahl Thriller #1)

The Relic Hunters Series
The Relic Hunters (Relic Hunters #1)
The Atlantis Cipher (Relic Hunters #2)

The Disavowed Series:
The Razor's Edge (Disavowed #1)
In Harm's Way (Disavowed #2)
Threat Level: Red (Disavowed #3)

The Chosen Few Series
Chosen (The Chosen Trilogy #1)
Guardians (The Chosen Tribology #2)

Short Stories
Walking with Ghosts (A short story)
A Whispering of Ghosts (A short story)

All genuine comments are very welcome at:

davidleadbeater2011@hotmail.co.uk

Twitter: @dleadbeater2011

Visit David's website for the latest news and information: davidleadbeater.com

Printed in Poland
by Amazon Fulfillment
Poland Sp. z o.o., Wrocław